MW01104077

Advance Praise for Chill of Deception:

"It doesn't seem like three years since I read my first Colbie Colleen cozy suspense mystery, and I love every one! Always entertaining, they're fun to read. Faith Wood is up there with the best mystery writers out there, and Chill of Deception doesn't disappoint!

—Marg Vanelk

"I look forward to the next Colbie Colleen book, and Chill of Deception is my favorite so far—although, all of them are great!

—Danielle Baker

"Another book by Faith Wood I couldn't put down!"

—Payton Cassadie

"Okay—so, if you haven't read any of Wood's books, get all of them, and start with the first book. I guarantee by the time you reach Chill of Deception, you're going to want more. And, more. And, more!"

—D.B. O'Connell

"All I can say is get them. All of them. Every Faith Wood book is a complete delight to read!"

—Mary Anne Kovacich

CHILL
OF
DECEPTION

CHILL
OF
DECEPTION

FAITH WOOD

Wood Media
British Columbia, Canada

ISBN: 978-1729625811

ISBN: 1729625819

Printed in the United States of America

DEDICATION

To all my readers—thank you!

CHAPTER

1

*I*t's one thing to take a few days off—or, a couple of weeks. But, three months? That's a whole different ballgame. After returning from Wyoming, Colbie and Brian toyed with the idea of accepting another case on the heels of their last one—when they thought about it, however, time to themselves sounded like a good idea. But, as twelve weeks rounded into thirteen, Colbie realized enough was enough—time to get back to work.

Brian, however, wasn't so sure. "It's not like we need the money," he commented as she flipped through her list of cases waiting to be solved. "Are you sure you're up to it?"

"Up to it? Why wouldn't I be up to it? Just because I took time off doesn't mean I compromised my faculties!"

She sat back in her chair, flashing a grin daring him to say something.

But, after all of their years together, he knew better. "Not going there," he commented, matching her grin with his own.

"Wise choice! So, what do you think? There are several cases, all of which are different . . ."

"Well—which one catches your attention? We talked quite a bit about the archaeological dig in Mexico when we got back from Wyoming—is it still on the table?"

Colbie flipped back to the first page of her notes, each possibility accompanied by a few paragraphs describing the nature of the case. "When I talked to the guy who contacted me, he sounded as if he had no clue as to what was going on—three workers disappeared and, if I remember correctly, they were never to be seen again . . ."

"Have you talked to him since?"

"Nope—and, he didn't make any effort to get in touch with me after our initial conversation. Maybe the situation resolved itself . . ."

"Could be they showed up—anyway, what else sounds interesting?"

She took a few moments before answering, trying to force her brain to make a decision. It wasn't her usual nature to be wishy-washy—normally, she had definitive opinions about which cases to accept. "I'm thinking I like this one . . ."

"Which is?"

"Savannah . . ."

"'Savannah' as in Georgia? Or, a 'savanna' as in Africa?"

"Georgia . . ."

"So—tell me . . ."

"Monroe Clyburn—he's the one who contacted me—is a high roller in the Savannah scene . . ."

"And?"

"According to my notes, when he first got in touch, his daughter—Mariska—was scheduled to attend a business meeting at their company, and never showed. That was four months ago . . ."

"Four months? Is he sure she's not just hanging with friends?"

"Without contacting him? Unlikely. But, I did some prelim research and, according to police reports, she's definitely listed as a missing person . . ."

"What kind of business?"

"I researched that, too—meds. Clyburn Pharmaceuticals was incorporated back in the fifties, and it's been family owned ever since." She paused as she tried to read the notes scratched in the margin of her legal pad. "Monroe Clyburn is the grandson of Chester Clyburn, and he took the reins of the company in two thousand. Since then, profits are up, and shareholders are pocketing some pretty hefty dividends . . ."

"And, his daughter? You said she disappeared after a company meeting—what's her position?"

"*Before* a company meeting—she's the Manager of Product Development . . ."

"So—she's in charge of new drug R and D? That sounds like a pretty high-up role . . ."

"Agreed—so, what's your gut? Should we accept the gig?"

"Do you think you have enough information to make a decision?"

"I think so—there's something about it that raises my antennae . . ."

Brian got up from the couch, heading for the kitchen. "Then, that's good enough for me! How soon?"

"Well, I need to get back with Mr. Clyburn, but I think we can be ready to head to Georgia by the middle of the month, don't you?"

"You make the decision," he conceded as he grabbed a slab of chocolate cake from the fridge. "Want some?"

She looked at the cake, knowing she should decline. "Are you kidding? Of course, I do!"

Colbie's timing was on point—by the middle of the following week, they packed, reviewed final instructions with Tammy for taking care of things at the office, and were on a jet slated to land at Savannah/Hilton Head Airport by mid-afternoon. As usual, Brian napped while Colbie added to her notes about the case—after several conversations with

Monroe Clyburn, she was convinced Mariska's disappearance was due to suspicious circumstances, but that was about all she knew. She wouldn't get a good handle on anything until they were on the ground, and she was on her own to investigate.

As she opened the case folder, Mariska Clyburn stared back at her from a classy, eight-by-ten photo, its quality rivaling that of a pricey professional. She looked like a model, but, from everything her father told Colbie, nothing was further from the truth—a science geek from the time she was twelve, Mariska had a head for anything medical, and she knew at a young age she wanted to be in the medical profession, but not necessarily a doctor. Driven to help society, when her dad offered her the opportunity to manage the product development division at the tender age of twenty-three, she jumped at the chance.

A chance ill-favored by those on the board who feared profits would suffer.

Nonetheless, within the first year of her tenure, company profits soared when Clyburn Pharmaceuticals announced a new medication was on the cusp of being available to the public. Even though the young Clyburn wasn't around for many of its test cycles, her tenacity when dealing with the feds regarding approval proved to be invaluable. There was something about her that made people sit up and take notice—and, it wasn't only because of her looks.

Colbie traced Mariska's last known locations with her index finger, lingering on the description of each time she was sighted the evening of December third—four-and-a-half months earlier. Hoping she could tap into a possible scenario of her disappearance, she closed her eyes, allowing her intuitive mind to surface, but, after only a few moments, it was a no go. For some reason, her frequencies felt blocked, and nothing was clear. Visions appeared vague and opaque, and the only thing she could make out before they faded was what appeared to be a bonfire—so, she filed it in the back of her mind to revisit later, if needed. She learned long ago her visions weren't constrained by time, making pinpointing specifics that much more difficult.

Her intuitive mind uncooperative, her thoughts fell to the interview list. The following day? Jason Marks— Mariska's boyfriend for the past two years. Those who knew them as a couple swore they got along well, and there was little in the way of domestic discord. *Well—there were a few knock-down, drag-outs,* she thought. *But, nothing serious if anyone is to believe Mariska's best friend—she says they loved each other.* She recalled Clyburn's first investigator's scribbled, nearly illegible notes—the only reason Colbie had them was because Monroe had the presence of mind to ask for every scrap of paper, receipt, and idea the investigator had as a result of the investigation.

Lucky.

For the most part, Marks was liked by his and Mariska's mutual friends. Hard working, they said, and he thought the world of Mariska. As a suspect in a murder? Never! *Still,* Colbie considered, *stranger things have happened . . .*

What she found interesting was the difference in the lovebirds' backgrounds. Mariska hailed from money— there was no doubt about that—and, Marks was from meager means. At first, people who knew them thought the relationship would never work simply based on economics— she had bucks, he didn't. But, as time passed, money didn't seem to matter to either of them, and they led their private lives according to budgets. Every once in a while, of course, Monroe chipped in for something they needed—such as a new car—but, that was only if they *really* needed it. Mariska wasn't one to ask for things, according to him, and she had a good sense for money—in other words, she tended not to spend what she didn't have.

That doesn't mean, however, Jason Marks followed the same economical way of life . . . With her years of experience, Colbie seldom believed what anyone told her until the information could be verified.

She also knew life was different behind closed doors.

As soon as they stepped off the plane, Colbie could feel the city's history, as well as its reputation for being hot and humid. A heaviness saturated the air, but Colbie was used to it, and it didn't bother her—it was the heat she wouldn't like. Life on the West Coast was damp, but never too hot. Savannah? When they landed, the temperature soared to eighty-five degrees with an eighty percent humidity, both setting records for the date. She felt as if a wet, wool blanket were wrapped around her, choking out every element of fresh air.

"Damn—it's hot here!" Brian dripped sweat as he loaded their luggage into a cab.

"No kidding! I can feel my hair frizzing . . ." She handed him the last carry-on bag, then climbed in the backseat as he closed the trunk. Moments later, they were one their way to one of Savannah's most historic, downtown inns.

Colbie gave the name of their hotel to the driver and, within the half hour, he rolled up in front of one of the most breathtaking, extraordinary buildings she could imagine. "Oh, my gosh! Brian! Look at this!"

"Holy crap! How much does this place cost?" He glanced at the building, then at the surrounding neighborhood. "I sure hope your client is paying . . ."

She shot him an exasperated look, then returned her focus to the inn. "He is—and, he's certainly sparing no expense!"

In the shade of blossoming magnolias, the cab driver hopped out and headed for the trunk, placing their luggage on the sidewalk. After Brian settled the bill, the driver bid them an enjoyable stay and, moments later, Brian and Colbie stood alone.

"This is incredible . . ."

Just then, the massive front door opened, and a young man in his twenties hurried to greet them. "We've been expecting you!" He shook hands with Colbie, then Brian. "I'll take your bags—Mrs. Davenport will show you to your room. She's waiting for you . . ."

They thanked him and, as soon as they stepped across the threshold, both gasped at the sheer beauty of the exquisite inn. Towering ceilings and floor-to-ceiling windows punctuated a sitting room filled with stunning colors meshing history and present with style and comfort. They soon discovered their room offered the same historic ambiance, inviting guests to enjoy stepping back in time.

"This place is amazing," Brian commented as he hoisted

his suitcase onto the bed, flipping open the locks.

Colbie agreed as she began hanging up her clothes. "Let's take a walk after we get settled . . ."

"An early dinner?"

"Sounds fabulous—anything with crab, and I'll be in hog heaven!"

"More so than if you're eating prime rib?"

"Well—maybe not. But, I still plan on eating my fill of it while we're here . . ."

"Speaking of that—did you factor in a particular time frame for our stay?"

Colbie shook her head. "Nope—you know as well as I, no matter what I plan, it gets blown out of the water almost immediately!"

"I've never had a mint julep—have you?"

Colbie placed her menu on the table, glancing at patrons enjoying a slight breeze on the patio. "Never—I'll stick with my glass of wine, thank you very much . . ."

She grinned at him, then took a sip. The woman sitting next to them sported a hat the size of Montana, and she exuded the feeling of old money. Old class. The old way of doing things. And, that's what Colbie found so fascinating— as with any city, there was a night life. Noise. Partying. Streets alive with people. But, as they sat amid the style of historic ancestry as the sun began to set, one would never know it existed.

"What are you having?" Brian glanced at her over the top of his menu.

"Crab stew—the stew at Cosmo's is really good, so it will be interesting to compare the two coasts."

"Good point—I'll have the same!"

After ordering, they nursed their drinks, talking about the case. Even though Colbie had more information than she usually got from clients, she still didn't have anything making Mariska's disappearance stand out.

"It's been nearly five-months since Clyburn's daughter disappeared," Brian observed. "I'm assuming you think she's dead after all this time . . ."

"I admit, that's what I thought before we left—now, I'm not so sure."

"Seriously? It's a long time to be out of touch with family and friends . . ."

"I know—but, now that we're here, something feels different."

"Different how?"

Colbie shuddered from an unexpected chill. "I don't know if I can put my finger on it, but it feels like . . . lies. I have a strong feeling we're going to have to dig deep to get to the truth . . ."

"Colbie! It's nice to meet you in person! I trust your accommodations suit you?" Monroe Clyburn extended his hand, his slow, southern drawl somehow more engaging in person.

"More than we expected! Thank you!" Colbie smiled, then turned her attention to a stunning, middle-aged woman who appeared the epitome of southern perfection. "And, you must be Mrs. Clyburn . . ."

"Indeed—please call me Agatha."

After brief introductions, they followed their hosts inside to the welcoming cool of air conditioning. Within minutes, the conversation turned to the reason Colbie and Brian were there.

"I trust you reviewed everything I sent—the notes, I mean . . ."

"I did—and, Brian and I reviewed them again during lunch."

"Excellent! What are your thoughts?" Monroe glanced at his wife, noticing she was hanging on Colbie's every word.

"Unfortunately, the reports of your former investigator were interesting, but not unlike many missing persons cases. Nothing really stood out as unusual . . ."

Monroe nodded. "Agreed—so, where are you going to start?"

"Well, I want to contact each person who was previously interviewed—I want to hear for myself their thoughts about why Mariska vanished . . ."

"And, while she's doing that," Brian interjected, "I'll talk to her colleagues at work."

"I'll take care of getting you in the door at the various departments—you'll begin tomorrow?"

"I'll be there at nine . . ."

"In the meantime," Colbie offered, "I'll start setting up interviews with Jason Marks and Mariska's personal friends." Colbie turned her attention to Agatha. "What do you think happened to your daughter?" For a moment, Monroe's wife seemed surprised at Colbie's direct approach, but realized quickly they needed someone tough in their corner if they were ever to get answers. Clearly, the woman from the West Coast didn't cotton to southern gentility.

"Honestly—I have no idea. She's such a good girl, and I can't think for the life of me who would want to do her harm." Her soft, southern accent was punctuated with the pain of considering she may never see her daughter again.

"Were you and she close?"

"As close as most mothers and daughters—we had our disagreements, but not so much after she graduated from college, and began working at the company."

"The company being Clyburn Pharmaceuticals?"

"Yes—she only had one other job before she accepted the position her father offered."

"Where was that?"

"Bio-Com Laboratory. She researched cell degeneration in individuals from ages twenty-five to forty-five . . .

CHAPTER

2

First days of a case always proved interesting—there were those who were willing to provide as much information as possible, while others remained reticent and guarded, unsure of divulging information to someone they didn't know. It made breaking the ice that much more difficult, and Colbie found herself looking for the one thing that would allow her entry into Mariska's inner circle of friends. There was a—privacy—regarded highly by most, and it took some convincing to schedule an interview.

"Jason Marks—he's first on my list . . ." Colbie buttered her croissant, then carefully added a dollop of peach jam.

"Check—I'm going to start with her colleagues at work, and I have three lined up for today. Are you going to try to get in more than one?"

"I hope so—I tried getting in touch with Christina Crossmore, but I haven't heard from her."

"And, she is?"

"Mariska's best friend since college—if there's anyone who knows about Mariska's private life, it Christina. That's according to Agatha . . ."

"Well, she ought to know . . ."

Monroe Clyburn was kind enough to provide Colbie with a driver—Brian, too—since they didn't know their way around the city. After considering the logistics of her investigation, she happily complied, and Kevin was assigned to take her wherever she wanted to go. Young and eager to climb the corporate ladder, he looked forward to it, thinking it might be a nice change of pace from the confines of his cubicle.

"Okay—you have the address. Are you familiar with where it is?" Colbie glanced at him, grinning. "You're supposed to know where everything is, you know . . ."

Kevin laughed. "Yes, Ma'am! I've lived in Savannah all my life—I'll be surprised if there's a place I can't find!"

"Do you know Jason Marks?" Normally, she wouldn't discuss any aspect of an investigation with anyone—except Brian—but, her gut was telling her Kevin might know him.

"Not really—he came into work a couple of times to meet up with Mariska, but that's about it. We don't travel in the same circles, if you know what I mean . . ."

"Really? I had the impression she and Jason were a frugal, young couple—you know, living on a budget . . ."

Kevin maneuvered the Mercedes into traffic, heading southeast. "I guess that depends on the amount of the budget, doesn't it?"

"Well, yes—you're right about that! So . . . did they flaunt their money?"

"No—it wasn't that. Mariska has too much class— Marks, on the other hand? I think he likes the fact his woman is filthy rich . . ."

Colbie thought about Kevin's comment as traffic whizzed by, drivers speeding toward private destinations. His perceptions of Mariska's and Jason's private lives were the opposite of what Monroe and Agatha told her. Understandable, because he's young—but, it did make Colbie wonder about Mariska's true relationship with her mother— were there things her mother didn't know?

"I'm not sure what you mean—did Jason Marks spend her money?"

Kevin glanced at her. "I don't know for sure—but, that's

what I heard . . ."

"From whom?"

Suddenly, he looked uncomfortable. "I'm not sure I should say . . ."

Colbie nodded. "I know—but, if something happened to Mariska, I need to know everything . . ."

The young intern from Clyburn Pharmaceuticals was quiet, silently weighing Colbie's words. "I know you're right. It's just . . ." Again, he fell silent.

"Just what, Kevin?"

"Oh—it's one of those situations you'd see on television. You know—partying. Everyone's hammered. People who have no business opening their mouths are jabbering about things they'll never remember in the morning . . ."

"Did you hear Marks say something?"

Kevin shook his head. "Not directly. But, a friend of mine was at a nightclub, and he mentioned he saw Mariska and Marks there. Marks was smashed out of his mind, and Mariska took off without him . . ."

"That's it?"

"Well, my friend said Marks went ballistic, and was asked to leave."

As Colbie listened, she had a feeling there was more to Kevin's story, but she also knew anything he told her was nothing more than hearsay. But, her driver's information wasn't necessarily inconsequential, and it certainly stirred Colbie's curiosity about how great Mariska's and Jason's relationship truly was . . .

Or, wasn't.

At ten-thirty, Kevin pulled into a gated community protecting residents from the unsavories who'd never understand the upper crust. *This seems a little ritzy for one who comes from such simple beginnings . . .* She watched Kevin's expression as he paid attention to road signs— of course, she didn't know him at all, but she thought she detected a shade of doubt.

He turned into a short, cobbled drive, then parked in front of two columns awaiting guests who sat atop the social ladder. "Fancy, schmancy . . ."

"That, it is!" Colbie paused. "Does this place strike you as a little weird? For someone who's supposed to come from very little, why am I meeting him here?"

"That's kind of what I was wondering . . ."

They sat for a moment—no more than a minute or two—until Colbie was ready to conduct the interview. "I don't know how long this will take, so make yourself comfortable!"

As she opened the car door, a young man in his mid-twenties strode toward her, extending his hand. "You must be Ms. Colleen—Jason Marks."

Colbie offered an engaging smile, accepting the handshake. "Please—call me Colbie!"

"I hope you didn't have any trouble finding this place— it's a little out of the way."

"Not at all—luckily, I have a driver who knows the city like the back of his hand!"

Jason was nothing like Colbie imagined. Of course, she had a photo of him and, clearly, he hadn't changed much since someone snapped it in early fall—three months before Mariska vanished. No—he looked the same, but she detected an instant sense of his being sly. Slick. Slithery.

Right from the git, she knew something wasn't quite right with Jason Marks, and Colbie didn't trust him for a minute. There was a polish to him—unusual for someone whose background didn't include reasonable economic means. From his attitude and clothing, as well as the home where Colbie was meeting him, Jason seemed to be a man who loved everything money could buy.

He squinted and leaned down, peering into the car from the passenger's window. "Kevin?"

"Hey, man—I'm sorry about Mariska . . ."

Jason nodded. "I'm hoping Colbie can help . . ."

Colbie stepped in, taking control of the conversation. "Well, that's why I'm here! How about if we get started?" She glanced at Jason, then at Kevin. "Kevin—why don't you join us?"

Although stunned by Colbie's invitation, he hopped out, then shook hands with the guy he met a few times at social functions and, sometimes, at Clyburn Pharmaceuticals. "Good to see ya . . ."

"Good! Shall we?" She gestured to Jason to lead the way.

Holy crap! Colbie couldn't help scanning the massive foyer as she crossed the threshold. *This looks like a freaking mausoleum!*

From the outside, the home appeared to be well maintained, and she expected the same as she entered. Instead, musty, vintage furniture greeted them, coupled with an odd fragrance she couldn't quite place.

Jason noticed her surprise. "You'd never think this is what it looked like on the inside, would you?"

Instinctively, Colbie mentally cataloged pictures quickly, as well as knickknacks, and everything else she could see within a few seconds. "Well—I have to admit, I'm a little . . ."

"Shocked?"

She looked at him, grinning. "I confess—I wasn't expecting this!"

"I know—I felt the same way. But, when my mom inherited this place from the old lady she took care of for years, we weren't quite sure what to do with it. We still don't know . . ."

"You don't live here?"

"Good God, no! Mariska and I have a place together closer to Savannah . . ."

"Then, why . . ."

"Why are you meeting me here? Because I'm meeting a friend of mine who's a contractor—he might have some ideas about what to do." He scanned the room, then gestured to a mid-century, Formica kitchen table. "Please—make yourself comfortable!"

Colbie chose a small, kitchen chair straight out of the fifties, while Kevin decided on one next to her. Jason sat across, not hesitating to look her in the eye.

"So, shoot—what do you want to know?"

His confidence was slightly unsettling and, as Colbie concentrated on him, she had the distinct feeling he was as duplicitous as the day is long. "Monroe Clyburn suggested we talk about Mariska's disappearance—did he explain why he brought me in on the case?"

"A little—he said you're an investigator from Seattle."

Colbie smiled. "That's right . . ." She turned to Kevin. "What did he tell you?" She figured if she were going to include her driver on case particulars, she may as well know how Monroe presented her expertise.

"Pretty much the same—then, he asked if I'd drive you around."

"Perfect! Then you know the basics of my work . . ."

Colbie doubted they were aware of the psychic component of her investigations, and she allowed her intuition to kick in as she sat across from the young man who definitely raised her antennae. He seemed harmless, but, perhaps, she was basing her assessment on what she learned from the first investigator's notes. When she tuned in, however, her intuition met a brick wall—something sparking further doubt, and she couldn't recall the last time she was unable to see or hear anything in her intuitive mind. It were as if everything were a blank slate, except for an almost imperceptible image of a tiny key.

"What do you think happened to Mariska," Jason asked.

"It's awfully early in my investigation, so I haven't formed an opinion on anything—that's why I'm talking to you."

He sat forward in his chair, hands clasped in front of him on the table. "Okay—what do you want to know?"

"Hold on . . ." Colbie reached into her messenger bag, withdrawing a small, digital recorder, then set it in the middle of the table. "Do you mind?"

"No—not at all."

He didn't miss a beat, she thought as she pressed the record button. "I finally gave up scratching my notes on tiny bits of paper," she laughed. "Now, I'm caught up with the times!"

"My mom still uses tiny pieces of paper . . ."

"She sounds like a woman I'd like . . ." She paused. "What does she think about Mariska's disappearance?"

"At first, she thought we must have had a fight, and Mariska took off . . ."

"Is that what you think?"

"I know that's not right!"

"Tell me . . ."

"Well, first off, we didn't have a fight, so that theory doesn't hold water. Second, we love each other—even if we did have a disagreement, nothing could make either one of us so angry, we'd have to leave . . ."

"What do you think happened to her?"

Jason's eyes brimmed with tears. "I have no idea . . ."

It was at that moment Colbie recognized he didn't have anything to do with Mariska's disappearance—that, however, didn't negate her initial impression. She still felt there was something sly about him.

Maybe it's because he has to be . . .

Brian crammed his legs under a tiny table positioned in the far corner of the lunchroom, listening to Mariska's middle-aged colleague confiding Mariska was far too young to have such a position at Clyburn. "Between you and me," she whispered, "it's nothing but nepotism!"

He cringed as his right calf began to cramp. "I take it you and Mariska didn't get along . . ."

"Oh, we got along just fine—it's just that . . ."

He waited. "It's just what?"

"Well, everyone knows I could do a better job—I wasn't the only one who was surprised when Clyburn announced her new position."

Brian suddenly found himself wishing he were in the middle of a root canal. "I understand. Do you have any thoughts about what happened to her?"

"Me? Good heavens, no! The only time I was around her was right here . . ."

"Nothing social?"

"Christmas parties—that's about it."

He paused a moment, then stood. "Thank you, Mrs. Parson—I appreciate your time. If you don't mind, will you please ask . . ." He checked his notes. ". . . Mr. Nixon to join me?"

"That's it?"

"Indeed—that wasn't too painful, was it?"

With a look of disappointment, Mrs. Parson scuttered out the door, casting a quick glance behind her as if someone cared about what she said, or did.

"Thank you," Brian called after her as he stretched out his legs underneath the table.

Moments later, a man pushing fifty stood at the doorway. "Clara said you want to talk to me . . ."

Brian stood, offering his best, genuine smile. "I do—I appreciate your making time."

"Ben Nixon . . ."

"Please—join me. I'll try not to keep you too long . . ."

"Keep me as long as you want! Staring at test tubes all day can get a little boring!" Nixon laughed easily, his demeanor casual and inviting. "What do you want to know?"

"Well—as you know, my partner and I are investigating Mariska Clyburn's disappearance . . ."

Nixon nodded. "If you ask me, the whole damned thing is weird . . ."

"Weird—in what way?"

"I'm not sure, exactly, but, after the first week of her being gone, everything returned to normal—like nothing ever happened. Roberts slipped into her position as if he were made for it, and no one mentions her name, anymore. It's as if she never worked here . . ."

Brian tapped his pencil on the table. "What about the people you work with? Surely there has to be some water-cooler gossip about her strange disappearance . . ."

"There was, but no one seemed to know anything—including me."

Brian scribbled a few notes on his small memo pad, then returned his attention to the man in a stiffly starched lab coat, no hair out of place. "What do you think?"

Nixon squared his eyes with Brian's. "I think someone did her in . . ."

"Someone you know?"

"Maybe." He paused. "Let me put it this way—I wouldn't be a bit surprised . . ."

CHAPTER

3

As with all of their investigations, Colbie and Brian had a tradition—checking in with each other throughout the day, and enjoying a glass of merlot as the sun went down.

Colbie closed her eyes as she made herself comfortable in a cushy, chaise lounge chair, wine glass in hand. Why she felt so tired, she didn't know—her day wasn't any different than any other when investigating. "I don't know about you, but I'm pooped!"

Brian laughed, swinging his feet onto a padded, wicker ottoman. "At least you didn't have your legs jammed underneath the tiniest table on the planet!"

"Oh, please—so, what did you find out? Anything?"

"Not at first—by the end of the day, I thought I'd lose my mind if I had to listen to one more person . . ."

"I know the feeling—anybody interesting?"

Brian nodded, popping a piece of cheese in his mouth. He chewed, swallowed, then grinned at Colbie. "Okay—only one guy piqued my interest—Nixon. Ben Nixon. It took him about two seconds after meeting me to tell me he thinks Mariska's disappearance is just plain weird . . ."

Colbie sat up, adjusting the back of the lounge chair so she had a good eye on him. "Weird how?"

"That's what I wanted to know—it seems Mariska's name was off the private office door within the week." He paused. "I gotta admit—that seems a little weird to me, too."

"Agreed . . ."

"He also said he thinks 'someone did her in'—that's a quote."

"Did he say who?"

"No, but when I asked if it were someone he knew, he said he wouldn't be surprised . . ."

Both sat for a few minutes, trying to unwind, thoughts racing. "What about you," Brian finally asked. "Anything interesting?"

"Interesting as in having a solid lead? No. But, the overall interview was interesting . . ."

"Hold that thought . . ." He plucked a few crackers from a vintage, silver tray, then topped each with a small wedge of sharp cheddar. Then, he made himself comfortable. "Okay—

shoot."

Colbie grinned. "Are you sure you're ready?"

"Yep—hit me . . ."

She laughed, arranging her summer skirt so it covered her legs. Oddly, there was a chill where she was sitting, even though the southern air dripped with humidity. "I think the biggest takeaway for me was realizing Jason Marks has absolutely nothing to do with Mariska's disappearance . . ."

"Really? Usually, you don't make a decision about a possible suspect so fast . . ."

"I know—but, I just don't think he has anything to do with it. At first, I misread his arrogance, but, as we talked, I realized he's probably not the sharpest knife in the drawer, and I don't see him hatching some sort of plot to kidnap . . ."

"Or, murder . . ." Brian thought for a second about her observations. "I don't know—I'm not sure I'd write him off so soon."

"I won't—but, I'm going to focus my attention elsewhere. Like on the Nixon guy you talked to—now, he interests me!"

"Same here—I think you should talk to him."

"Me, too. Will you set it up for me, please?"

He saluted. "Yes, Ma'am!"

As the air started to cool slightly, Brian reached for Colbie's hand—there they sat, hand-in-hand, perfectly in tune. Perfectly satisfied.

Perfectly happy.

"Did I tell you I heard from my parents?" Brian pulled the covers back on their bed, plumping both pillows.

Colbie stopped brushing her teeth, staring at him in disbelief. "You're kidding! Where are they?"

"Some place I can't pronounce—but, apparently, they're going to be stateside at the end of the month."

Colbie remembered the last time she had anything to do with his parents, years earlier. They never took interest in her even when Brian made it clear they were going to be together for the rest of their lives—and, they certainly had little patience for anything in his life. "Where will they be?"

Brian chuckled. "That's what's strange—Seattle, of all places!"

"Seriously? Are you going to see them?"

He thought for a moment. "Maybe—I haven't decided. It'll depend on how the investigation's going . . ."

"Well, at least you don't have to decide immediately—it shouldn't be too difficult to get a plane ticket last minute . . ."

Exhausted, they finally fell into bed, each making silent plans.

It was a pretty darned good first day.

Agatha Clyburn was an interesting woman—at least, some thought so. Born into bucks, she never wanted for anything, and her father was willing to provide whatever she needed in the way of clothes. Travel. New cars. Oh, yes—it was a life craved by many, yet achieved by few, and the youngest addition to the Culpepper clan way back when didn't feel guilty at all when she arrived for the first day of school in the best patent leather shoes money could buy.

But, it was the ubiquitous pony that was her was first clear recollection of the perks of privilege. Her best friend wanted one in the worst way, and there was more than a shred of jealousy when Agatha got one, and she didn't. Icy glares at recess coupled with refusing to sit with one another at the lunchroom table served to fracture their friendship and, by second grade, it proved irretrievable. The split was permanent, and both considered it a good thing when Agatha's parents sent her to a private school rooted in good manners, education, and anything involving money.

As you might imagine, such a lifestyle didn't endear her to those less fortunate, but, truth be known, she didn't give a rat's ass about them. Her life had always been about money, and it would always be about money. Nothing more. Nothing less. So, it was a good day when Monroe Clyburn waltzed into her life on a lazy summer afternoon after playing nine holes in Savannah's sweltering sun. A few golf games and mint juleps later, they were an item, both understanding they would always—in each other's lives—rate second to the almighty dollar.

A perfect match.

Interestingly, however, Savannah society didn't interest either of them. They preferred to keep their personal lives to themselves and, month by month, year after year, they quietly went about the business of building a pharmaceutical empire. Offers of buyouts were usual, but Monroe didn't have an interest in letting anyone else benefit from his hard work. "I'm already filthy rich," he told his wife after an offer to buy out Clyburn Pharmaceuticals hit the conference room table. "Why do I need to sell?"

Agatha wasn't quite so sure. In her mind, one could always use more money, and she couldn't conceptualize having enough. Still, she acquiesced to her husband's professional wisdom, and the company was destined to remain in Clyburn hands.

Monroe's legacy.

As the Clyburn matriarch, it was her job to make certain the household ran smoothly, something that was difficult to maintain with three children even though Mariska's brothers were considerably older. Naturally, she had help, but there was still a significant amount of stress when it came to raising a family. Keeping that in mind, she made sure her children wanted for nothing, and Monroe's job was to pay for everything. Private schools, private this, private that—all in the name of preparing her children for the world she knew.

That's why she was so surprised—shocked was more like it—when Mariska announced she wanted to attend college close to home. "Are you certain, Mariska," her mother asked in her soft, southern drawl. "We have connections at the finest schools . . ."

Even so, Mariska declined, and it was something her mother never understood. She also never understood what her daughter saw in Jason Marks—to her way of thinking, he wasn't good enough for Mariska, and she vowed—the first time she met him—to do everything in her power to make her daughter see the light. Their relationship was often the topic of pillow talk, and Monroe confided to his wife he didn't really understand her, either. She, however, rightfully pointed out he didn't need to understand her—he only needed to make sure she had everything she wanted.

What Agatha didn't understand was there was a part of Monroe needing to keep his third child close. It was always his dream to have Mariska take over the pharmaceutical business, and he knew he could trust her with what he took so long to build—and, it was more than he could say for his sons. He and Agatha raised her to be reliant on money for they knew with such a mindset Mariska would always need to pursue something.

Too bad Mariska didn't get the memo.

When entering college, she promised herself she'd study hard, laying claim to spotless grades, as well as the admiration of her friends and professors. No one knew—unless she told them—she came from money, and that was the way she wanted it. Life seemed more genuine, and she thoroughly enjoyed hanging out with friends, stuffing her face with pizza every once in a while without worrying about what her parents would think if they knew she was poo-pooing the upper crust.

By the time Mariska graduated college and completed her master's degree in pharmaceutical engineering, she was well on her way to becoming a force within the industry. Several companies vied for her attention, and she spent her first years out of school at a well-known bio research firm dabbling in cell degeneration. Her research was kept close to the vest by company execs, and they counted on her to crack the code for the drug that would help those afflicted with muscular dystrophy, and other neurological disorders. Their interest in such a drug was personal, and those working at Bio-Com never knew why there was so much emphasis placed on the new drug. Company policy, however, dictated employees didn't need to know—and, that's precisely the reason Mariska chose to accept her father's offer to manage the product development division at Clyburn—she was tired of the pressure.

And, disrespect.

After Mariska's slipping seamlessly into the swing of things, Monroe Clyburn recognized what his daughter brought to the company was invaluable. She shared with him the importance of her work at Bio-Com, and he gave her the full go-ahead to continue her research at Clyburn's.

Nine months later?

Vanished.

Christina Crossmore sat across from Colbie at a small table by the front door of the coffee shop—it was the only one available, and certainly not the best seating arrangement.

"So—how long have you known Mariska?" Colbie took a sip of her iced tea, an unusual choice for her at nine-thirty in the morning.

"Since college—we met when both of us entered the engineering school."

Colbie sat back, focusing her full attention on the woman seated across from her. "I'm going to get right to the point—what do you think happened to Mariska?"

Christina looked slightly stunned by Colbie's blunt approach—it wasn't the southern way. "Well, I'm not sure— it's not like her to stay away, so I can only conclude something is amiss . . ."

Colbie tried not to smile at Christina's manner and phrasing—she was the epitome of southern charm and breeding. "When was the last time you saw her?"

"Last Thanksgiving—I remember it well because she and Jason were having some sort of row, and she didn't want him with her for the family dinner."

"Do you know why?"

"Not really—but, I do seem to recall she mentioned her mother didn't want him there. Something about his not fitting in with family . . ."

As Christina talked, Colbie noticed the southern façade slowly begin to vanish, akin to a snake sloughing its skin. "What about Jason Marks? What do you know of him? What do you think of him?"

By the time she got the last question out of her mouth, Christina Crossmore was nothing more than a young woman who couldn't figure out what happened to her best friend. Gone was the charm, and alluring southern accent.

"Jason? I never liked him—and, I don't know what Mariska saw in him!"

"But, if I recall correctly, that isn't what you told the first investigator . . ." Colbie flipped through her notes, finally locating where Christina said he and Mariska got along just fine. "Here it is—he reported you thought Jason and Mariska got along well, and you liked him . . ."

Christina's eyes turned dark, recalling the conversation. "If you're talking about that doofus Kingston, he doesn't know his ass from . . ." She paused, checking her criticism. "I'm sorry . . ."

"Good heavens—there's nothing to be sorry about! But, clearly what you told the first investigator isn't what you really think or feel . . ." She waited. "Will you tell me?"

Mariska's friend thought for a moment. "Okay—the truth is I never like Jason Marks from the first day I met him, and I told her so. 'He's not right for you,' I said, but she refused to listen."

"Do you recall where they met?"

"I think he was fixing her car . . ."

"He's a mechanic?"

"Yep—I'm not sure he still is, though."

"Why do you say that?"

"Because her mother made it clear he wasn't good enough for her . . ."

Colbie glanced out the window, noticing skies turning grey as if a cloudburst were imminent. "Agatha said that?"

"More than once . . . she never let Mariska forget it!"

Colbie's memory cycled back to her first conversation with Monroe and Agatha in person, both playing the part of distraught parents. *Perhaps,* she thought, *Agatha's and Mariska's relationship wasn't as strong as she said . . .*

It wasn't the first time she had that thought.

"And, lately," Christina continued, "they were fighting a lot."

"Agatha and her mother?"

"No—Jason and Mariska."

That was news! Jason told Colbie they had their disagreements, but nothing unusual. "What did they fight about?"

"Well—I think it was about money, mostly. Mariska was never one to spend money needlessly even though she's rich. Jason, on the other hand, likes to spend every dollar he has. And, he likes to spend Mariska's money, too . . ."

Their conversation continued for another hour, Christina filling Colbie in on the months leading up to Mariska's disappearance. By the end of their time together, Colbie's first impression—and, perhaps, hasty—opinion of Jason Marks was becoming a bit more opaque. Not that he was at the top of her list—there really wasn't a list, so far— but, she could well imagine he'd claim that position before too long.

As they parted on the sidewalk in front of the coffee shop, Colbie watched the tall, lanky woman fold herself into a snazzy sports car, then tap a number into her cell. Unsure of what to think of Mariska's best friend, she was quickly figuring out she hadn't heard the complete truth from anyone.

Including Monroe and Agatha Clyburn.

CHAPTER

4

onroe Clyburn stood at the window of his office watching a funeral procession crawl past his building. By the time the last limo inched by, his thoughts turned from problems of work to the investigation. When he first met Colbie Colleen in person, he didn't see much difference between her and any other investigator—and, he used plenty of them over the last decades. It wasn't so much the way she looked—it was her demeanor. Then, noticing a strength about her he found subtly unsettling, he made a mental note to keep track of every aspect of her work.

"Mr. Clyburn?"

Monroe turned and headed to his desk, briefly making eye contact with the young man standing in the doorway. He made it a policy over the years anyone could talk to him, including those in the mail room, if need be. He never wanted to be the type of boss who extricated himself from lower-level Clyburn Pharmaceuticals employees—besides, it was much easier to keep tabs on the goings on in each department. So, it wasn't a surprise when someone showed up at his office door. It was irregular, he knew, but the practice served its intended purpose on more than one occasion.

"Anything to report," he asked, motioning for his guest to sit.

"Nothing, Sir. Things are going according to plan . . ."

Clyburn thought about that for a moment, then reached into his desk drawer for a sealed envelope. "Give this to Roberts," he directed.

A pause.

"Now . . ."

Throughout the morning, Brian kept in touch with Colbie, agreeing to meet back at the inn by four-thirty or five that evening. Most of his research could be done on the Internet, but he always made it a point to visit a city or town's main library during an investigation—the one south of the city seemed a good place to start. His focus?

Monroe Clyburn.

Before he dove in to public records, he already knew the Clyburn Pharmaceuticals heir was a man to take seriously. Preliminary online investigation searches didn't yield much, but there were a few quotes from colleagues mentioning how serious Clyburn was about his family business. One article recounted how Clyburn raised quite a stir when he refused buyout offers—and, not particularly known for his good natured sense of humor, there was an invincibility to Monroe's personality that wasn't well received by those who wanted him to do things their way.

But, that wasn't unusual. From the time Monroe Clyburn was old enough to sit on his daddy's knee while he worked to make his company great, he knew he wanted to be just like him—strong. Stolid. Staunch. So, when middle school rolled around, it came as no surprise when the boy who was big for his age snagged the role of quarterback for one of the best park league teams.

That's when he became a leader.

High school was no different. Monroe continued to impress those who had an interest in him for sports scholarships, but his allegiance never wavered. With taking over the family business squarely in his sights, he tended to prove his worth in the classroom rather than on the football field. It was probably for the best—even though he possessed strong leadership qualities, he was a quiet, reserved young man, and he was most confident when keeping to himself in the science lab.

He always thought it was his love for chemistry and business that guided him to the university offering the best programs. While there, he spent most of his time studying, but, when he met Agatha?

Well, things changed.

Together, they planned their lives, both certain they wanted to assume responsibility for the family business when the time came. Agatha was welcomed into the Clyburn clan, Monroe's parents instantly recognizing she was the type of girl their son needed as a wife. Classy and well-educated, she would represent the Clyburns with distinction, and they didn't hesitate to let her know she was an asset, always to be at Monroe's side.

And, that's the way it was until the clock ticked into the new century. Chester Clyburn handed the reins to his grandson shortly before his passing, and Monroe, Agatha, and their two boys were enjoying the life they were meant to live.

Things, however, weren't quite so rosy when Mariska popped into the picture. Monroe thought his parenting days were coming to a halt since the boys were nearing college age—and, independence. Not theirs—his. He was a good father, but he didn't adjust well when it came to spending quality time with his kids. That required a balancing act between work and home, so, most of the time, he opted to take care of things at work—until Agatha called him on his B.S. "If you think I'm raising these kids alone," she threatened, "you can think again . . ." Since then, they enjoyed designated family nights and, Monroe had to admit, they were good for him, as well. But, there was one thing that would never change.

His bold, uncompromising love for money.

Once he felt the reins of power in his hands, something clicked, and he realized he was to be the catalyst for higher earnings, as well as greater bottom-line profits. Throughout the years when Mariska was in high school and college, his efforts paid off as Clyburn Pharmaceuticals reached unheard of sales pinnacles, rocketing off of their previous charts. Of course, he always touted the increase was due to everyone's efforts, but, even the newest employees knew it was because of Monroe. His quiet strength led employees to do their best and, when he finally convinced his daughter to join the ranks, he knew the company's success would continue to grow.

He was right, too.

It wasn't long until she took him into her confidence when discussing her work with Bio-Com. For as careful as her previous company's execs were, they failed to have her sign a confidentiality agreement—an egregious error. And, although she respected their unyielding positions while they operated their corporation, she really wanted to continue her work under the watchful eye of her father.

A business match made in heaven? Not really. Monroe found his daughter to be different at work than she was at home. Granted, they didn't spend much time together once she headed to college, but, he truly was surprised when he learned of the seriousness of her relationship with Jason Marks, as well as her dogged approach to anything pharmaceutical.

Agatha often reminded him Mariska was certainly her father's daughter, and Monroe wasn't quite sure how to take her comment. A good thing, he hoped, but, if anyone knew the truth about how he ran his business? Let's just say they wouldn't be so enamored of Mr. Monroe Clyburn.

Not so enamored, at all . . .

"I don't think I've ever been so hot and sweaty in my life," Brian groaned as he scooted a chair out from the table and sat, adjusting his ball cap while wiping his brow. "I'll take rain any day . . ."

Colbie laughed, then caught their server's attention. "A tall, cool drink for both of us, please—what do you recommend?"

The server rattled off several house favorites, but both ultimately decided on mint juleps. "I feel as if I need to be at a horse race," Brian joked as he took the first sip. "Holy crap!"

"Stronger than you thought?" Colbie couldn't help grinning as Brian set the drink on the table.

"You could have warned me!"

"How was I supposed to know? I've never had one, either!" With that, she took a tentative sip, determined she wouldn't fall prey to the same reaction. "Holy shit . . ."

"Told ya . . ."

For the next thirty or so minutes, they sipped and talked, recapping events of their day. Brian recounted what he learned about Monroe, calling into question something he and Colbie hadn't previously discussed. "What about the boys?"

"What boys?"

"Mariska's brothers—we haven't talked about them

since you accepted the case." He glanced at her as she plucked a cold-water prawn from its nest of shaved ice. "What are your thoughts?"

Colbie's brows arched as she thought about his question. "I'm planning on talking to them, but I think they're not a very strong part of the picture. Monroe and Agatha didn't talk about them much, and I certainly got the feeling Mariska is the golden child."

Brian nodded. "Same here. But, when I researched Monroe today, there was barely a mention of them—that makes me wonder why."

"Me, too . . ." She flipped through her notepad. "Marcus and Melbourne—both are quite a bit older than Mariska, and I recall Agatha's telling me raising three children while Monroe was busy at work was a real source of contention."

"She said that?"

"Yep—and, from the disdainful look on her face, I have a feeling she probably wouldn't do it again."

Brian was quiet, as he snagged another prawn. "Doesn't that make you wonder?"

"That depends—wonder what?"

"About why the brothers aren't a topic of conversation— maybe there's bad blood."

"Maybe . . ."

"There's always the possibility they have something to do with their sister's disappearance."

Colbie nodded. "You're right—I'll bump up talking to them to the first thing next week."

And, there they sat. Enjoying the setting sun. The cooling air.

Each other.

"I'm sorry for your loss . . ."

Monroe's head snapped up, glaring at the man standing in front of his desk. "My loss? What loss?"

"Mariska—I can't imagine . . ."

For the first time, Monroe exploded, the pressure of his daughter's disappearance finally taking its toll. He leapt to his feet, slamming his fist on the fine, dense mahogany. "How dare you! You speak as if my daughter is dead!"

The man didn't flinch. "I apologize—I didn't mean . . ."

"Get out!"

The man didn't move.

"I said, get out!" Monroe's lips contorted as rabid anger began to consume him. He wasn't used to being defied by anyone, let alone someone who was mostly inconsequential.

Silence.

Without a word, the man pivoted, and headed for the

door. Monroe watched, hatred seething through every fiber. *How dare he! That son of a bitch!*

As the door closed, he sat, trembling. Was Mariska's death something he should consider? Colbie and Brian had been on the case for nearly a month and, as far as he could see, there wasn't much to show for the money he was spending. He religiously combed her notes at the end of each week, familiarizing himself with the elements of the investigation. Of course, she informed him it could take a good while before learning what happened to his daughter, and it was a risk he was willing to take. Still, four weeks into it? *Surely, she must have some idea . . .*

Marcus Clyburn undeniably had a good handle on life. Many years older than his sister, he chose to distance himself from the family business, even though he enjoyed the perks it provided. Tall and broad, he obviously took care of himself, and Colbie suspected there was little want for anything but perfection. Arrogant? Definitely. Spoiled? Indisputably. A killer? *Only time will tell,* Colbie thought as she took a chair in the well-appointed sitting room. His taste and style mirrored his mother's, and Colbie was sure the cheapest thing in the room cost thousands.

After meaningless pleasantries, as well as accepting the offer of a sweetened iced tea, Colbie dove in, feet first. "What do you think happened to your sister?"

Marcus grinned. "You don't waste any time, do you?"

"Well, Mr. Clyburn, there isn't any time to waste—the longer we don't hear anything . . ."

"Oh, please—it's been nearly six months! Next week is the middle of June for God's sake! If nothing else, Ms. Colleen, let's be honest with each other . . ."

Marcus's wife took her place beside him. "What my husband is trying to say . . ."

"Don't speak for me! I'm perfectly capable of wrangling my own thoughts, and presenting them for consideration!"

Properly admonished, she sat back, casting Colbie an apologetic glance.

Time to step in. "I gather by your comment, you believe your sister is no longer living . . ."

His face darkened as he fidgeted with the glass in his hand. "I don't know . . ."

It was then Colbie felt an overwhelming sense of grief. For all of his bravado, Marcus Clyburn was filled with a sense of dread and uncorroborated knowledge. Without asking, she knew he thought he would never see his sister again.

"You must have some idea—is there anything you can tell me that will help in my investigation?"

Marcus shrugged. "Mariska never confided in me—we weren't close. In fact, the last time I saw her was two years ago at a family function—mother insisted I attend. If she hadn't done so, I most likely would have passed on the festivities."

"You don't get along with your family?"

"Not really—although, I can't say we don't 'get along.' We simply have different ways of perceiving life . . ."

Colbie glanced around the room. It looked to her as if Marcus Clyburn lived a life of opulence, his wife appearing as if she stepped right out of the *Stepford Wives*. Not a hair out of place. Fresh lip gloss carefully applied to her full lips. *A somewhat vacuous look*, Colbie thought, as she took note of the woman sitting next to her husband.

Perhaps a different tact. "Tell me about Mariska—I'm sure you have memorable stories . . ."

He glanced at her, a nasty look in his eyes. "Not really— I'm older than she, so our paths never crossed much as she was growing up. Mother made certain of that . . ."

"In what way?"

"Oh, c'mon, Ms. Colleen—surely you've picked up on the fact Mariska was the . . . favored child. Oh, my brother and I wanted for nothing—except parental affection—and, we learned to make that situation work."

Normally, Colbie would invite someone she interviewed to call her by her first name. In her current circumstance, however, she didn't offer the familiarity. Her voice softened as she asked her next question. "I can't imagine how that made you feel—did Mariska make it a point to get to know you better as she matured?"

"Mariska? Hardly—she was rightly spending time with her friends, as well as in the lab. There was little time for family and, to be honest, I didn't much care."

Marcus's wife stood, crossing to a vintage buffet. "Do you care for a refill, Ms. Colleen," she asked, picking up the crystal pitcher.

Colbie declined, watching her pour another glass for herself, as well as her husband. Then she refocused her attention on Marcus. "Again—what do you think happened to Mariska?"

Perhaps it was her imagination, but Colbie felt the air thicken with deception. Not a vision, but more of a feeling—Marcus Clyburn and his wife were hiding something, and Colbie refused to believe otherwise.

CHAPTER

5

assius Sprague headed the conference table, twelve
key execs seated comfortably distanced from each
other. The CEO called the emergency meeting
that afternoon and, when that happened, everyone knew it
couldn't be good.

Eyes turned toward him as he cleared his throat. "It's
come to my attention Monroe Clyburn hired a world-class
private investigator to search for his daughter."

No response.

"In light of that," he continued, "I'm ordering you to cease
continuing her research and development for combating cell

degeneration."

"Permanently?" The brusque head of operations glanced at his colleagues, wondering if they, too, were considering if Sprague were out of his mind. "We spent a bundle, so far— this decision will cost Bio-Com a fortune!"

Sprague shot him a steely glare before catching the eyes of everyone around him. "I don't give a damn how much it costs . . . do it!"

That was it. Everyone filed out with the exception of the main guy from IT. As the door closed, he sat catty-corner from his boss, awaiting explanation for the silent signal he was to stay.

"Get rid of everything . . ."

"Wiped?"

"BleachBit, if you have to . . ."

Nothing more passed between them—except silent acknowledgment of the need for expediency.

Kevin pulled out of Marcus Clyburn's drive, turning left toward the main road. "Now where?" He glanced at Colbie as she studied her notes.

She checked her watch. "Melbourne is kind enough to see us today, if we have time. It's only two-thirty, so let's go for it . . ."

"Address?"

Colbie rattled off the street and number, prompting Kevin to turn right at the next light to head the opposite direction. "Is it far?"

"Not really—thirty minutes on a good day." He paused, unsure if he should ask his next question. "How'd it go?"

"With Marcus?"

He nodded. "I know it's none of my business, so, if I'm stepping out of bounds, just let me know . . ."

Colbie was silent, thinking she may have made a mistake allowing him to sit in on her interview with Jason Marks. She regretted it afterward, but not until Brian brought her poor decision to the forefront of their conversation. "That was a huge risk," he admonished. "I hope it doesn't come back to bite you in the ass . . ."

Maybe he's right. "Unfortunately, you're correct—and, I'm not comfortable discussing Mr. Clyburn's private business with anyone, let alone someone who works for him." She paused. "That said, Kevin, I never should have allowed you to be in on my interview with Jason Marks. It's best if we stick to a driver-passenger relationship. We can talk about anything except the case—agreed?"

Kevin's face flushed with embarrassment. "Agreed!"

Colbie grinned. "I knew you'd understand—thanks."

He flashed her a genuine smile—anything she wanted was okay with him.

The thirty-minute estimate for arriving at Melbourne's was slightly skewed due to lane work on the main highway. By the time they arrived, it was past three-thirty, and all Colbie could do was hope he'd understand. Based on her conversation with Marcus, she wasn't sure what to think about any of the Clyburns, including Mariska and her two brothers. As many weeks as they were into the investigation, neither she nor Brian were where they should be—which, made her question why. Red herrings?

Maybe.

"This is it?" Colbie scanned the front yard littered with toys, bushes in front of the picture window in dire need of a trim, and water. Standing shriveled and stiff—their lives undoubtedly cut short by lack of interest—some limbs were snapped off, left to dangle precariously.

"Yep . . ." He checked the GPS on the dashboard. "Right on the money . . ."

"Really . . ."

She sat, the obvious dichotomy between Marcus and Melbourne staring her down. Where Marcus's home was opulent and well-kept, his brother's was located on a side street littered with lower middle class—evidenced by a hole in the fence serving as a portal for neighborhood critters to explore and do their business.

Still stunned by the scene before her, Colbie got out and stood by the car, her intuition in full swing. She watched the vision play out in her mind—a locket. Wisps of dark hair laying against a bright-white background. Then, a peacock feather.

"Ms. Colleen?"

Colbie opened her eyes, a small, timid man standing in front of her. "I'm sorry—I got caught up in my thoughts for a moment!" She extended her hand. "Colbie Colleen."

The man smiled, showing a tobacco-stained row of irregular teeth. "Melbourne Clyburn . . ."

After apologizing for being late, he invited her inside, settling at the tiny kitchen table in the tiny house. "In order to save time," Colbie began, "I'll get right to the point—what do you think happened to Mariska?"

Melbourne was quiet for a moment, eyes downcast as he chewed on the index fingernail of his right hand. "I don't know . . ."

She watched, instantly understanding the man sitting with her was completely disconnected from the Clyburn family—and, wealth. "When was the last time you saw her?"

"Two years ago . . ."

"Where?"

"At a family gathering—but, I didn't want to go."

Then, Colbie got it—before her was a man scared of his own shadow. "Did you have fun when you saw her last," she asked, her tone gentle and coaxing.

"Yes—but, then she left with that guy . . ."

"Jason Marks?"

Melbourne nodded.

"What do you think of him? Do you think they got along?"

He looked up, locked eyes with hers, his tone suddenly cold. "How should I know?"

Astonished, she watched Melbourne's face change. His demeanor shifted and, without warning, he was a man who commanded respect. A man who was up to settling a score.

A man who skyrocketed to the top of Colbie's list.

"I'm going to be later than I thought . . ." She glanced at Kevin. "Probably within the hour—traffic's a nightmare!"

"Check—oh, I heard from my parents. They'll be in Seattle at the end of the week . . ."

Colbie straightened a little as a chill swept through her. "Are you going to meet up?"

"Well—I think I should, don't you?"

She was quiet for a moment, thinking about the last time Brian saw his parents—as far as she remembered, there wasn't a last time. "If you think it's a good idea, I'm with you—but, I think you should go by yourself. I'm knee deep, and I don't want to lose my momentum . . ."

"I get it—I'll only be gone a few days. No more than three, most likely . . ."

After discussing possible flights to the West Coast, Colbie rang off. She was careful not to discuss the case in front of Kevin, and she wasn't particularly comfortable with his hearing her personal, private plans. But, as she glanced at him, he seemed not to notice, keeping his eyes on the road.

If Brian were her chauffeur—as he usually was during investigations—they could prep, plan, and prioritize while driving. Without that, Colbie felt an unfamiliar distance—not necessarily with Kevin, but with the situation. When she was speaking to Brian moments before, she had a strong sense of fire—an explosion—but, of course, she couldn't tell Kevin about it, so she'd have to wait until she returned to the inn to discuss it.

For the first time, the trip back to Savannah was filled with a tension she couldn't explain. As she tried to tune in on her driver, a solid, black wall greeted her, as if to say he was off limits. *Weird*, she thought, as she tried again.

Then, a vision slammed her intuitive mind, full force! She felt a singeing, scorching heat as her thoughts spiraled, skewing every perception. Again! And, again! It hit with such force, she couldn't think of anything, but the vision before her.

Then, it was gone.

Surfacing to her conscious mind, she glanced at Kevin—he appeared completely unaware. *Thank God,* she thought as she tried to compose herself. In all of her years as a psychic investigator—since childhood, really—she could remember only a few times such power coursed through her, leaving her breathless as she regained conscious thought.

And, she didn't like it.

The vision filled her with soul-searing darkness, its presence a loneliness she could only imagine. Slowly, it filled her being, taunting her as it reached the top of her head, brushing away her soundless cries for help.

Never had she felt so alone.

Mornings in Savannah were usually sun-drenched and beautiful, but, when they awakened the following morning, thick, smoky clouds greeted them, convincing Colbie and Brian it was the kind of day to stay indoors, hatching plans.

By ten-thirty, a steady rain slapped against their inn window, making progress with interviews scheduled for the day off the table. Colbie offered to conduct them via the Internet, but reception during nature's onslaught offered little hope of an acceptable connection.

"You know what I think," Brian commented as he settled on the couch in his sweats and slippers.

"What's that?" Colbie adjusted her glasses as she opened her laptop.

"I think we should take the day off . . ."

"What? Why?"

He looked at her over the rim of his coffee mug. "Because we're working all the time! When was the last time you and I took a proper day off, thinking of ourselves instead of our clients?" He waited about a second for an answer. Too late. "I'll tell you when—not since we started this investigation, that's for sure!"

He meant his tone to be teasing, but, somehow, it seemed laced with an unsettling truth.

Colbie took off her glasses, shooting him a look. "Are you serious?"

"Well—yeah. You work too hard, and I think we should take some time to gear down." He looked out the window. "And, today seems like the perfect day . . ."

She stared at him for a second, then burst out her recognizable, delightful laugh. "Okay, okay! A day off it is!" With that, she pushed out her chair from the suite table and tackled him on the couch, smothering his face with kisses. "Is this what you had in mind?"

He laughed, pulling her close. "Yep—exactly!"

A week of strong, persistent cloudbursts delayed flights, and it wasn't until the last minute that Brian boarded a flight bound for Washington. He and Colbie went over last-minute plans for the investigation, knowing full well he wouldn't be spending much time with his parents. That allowed him time to investigate from his hotel—and, why wouldn't he? He and they were well aware their meeting wasn't about loving, family time.

It was about obligation.

Colbie watched as he climbed into a cab, checking her watch to make certain he was allowing enough time for check-in. "I'll call right before I board," he promised, flashing her a toothy grin.

Moments later, she watched the taxi round the corner.

She was on her own.

CHAPTER

6

She thought about discussing Melbourne's interesting personality transformation with his father, quickly deciding it was more prudent to keep observations to herself. But, what she witnessed was more than fleeting and, by the time she left the tiny, unkempt house, she was certain there was more to Melbourne Clyburn than she initially perceived.

Throughout their time together, Melbourne maintained he knew little about family business details, his demeanor morphing from the timid, little man who met her on the sidewalk to someone confident, and unflappable. Not only that, he vehemently denied knowing anything about his sister's disappearance. Still, she found him to be strange.

Quirky. There was no familial resemblance to Agatha or Monroe, although there might have been a smidge of Marcus in him. The only thing she determined instantly was they shared a common denominator—smarts. It was clear Melbourne was graced in the brains department— articulate and well-educated, his delivery could use a little work, but, what Colbie found interesting was his complete refusal to talk about his brother. At the mention of Marcus's name, Melbourne clammed up, and Colbie thought briefly it seemed a classic case of an older brother traumatizing a sibling. Yet, she felt there was something more going on, reminding herself to talk to Brian about it when he called that evening.

After a quick bite to eat at a street-side deli, she was back in her room at the inn before sunset. *It's strange not having him here,* she thought as she wrapped up for the day, organizing her files and schedule for the following morning. Again, she considered the case somewhat stymied, but not for lack of trying—for the last couple of weeks, she had the distinct feeling she was being purposefully led in the wrong direction.

Knowing Brian would call at any moment, she made a mental note of the things she needed to discuss, turned on the television for the late-night news, then showered and got ready for bed. Again, she thought of how much she relied on his being there when they were on an investigation—it was lonely without him.

As she adjusted the volume, Colbie watched a young reporter take her mark in front of the camera, a strong wind blowing long strands of hair across her face. "At eleven-fifteen this morning," she began, "a flight originating in Savannah, bound for Seattle, crashed into the side of a mountain not far from its destination." The reporter paused to swipe at piece of windswept hair. "According to the NTSB, there are no survivors . . ."

Colbie watched dying embers of the mangled jet behind the reporter and, in that instant, her stomach lurched as she realized the significance of the explosion she saw in her vision.

Eyes glued to the smoldering jet, she listened as the reporter described the scene.

Nothing, but wreckage.

CHAPTER

7

Three months passed, Colbie's heart aching each morning as she opened her eyes to when she closed them again at night. A searing, scorching grief laid claim to her soul, seldom allowing her a moment's peace—and, her days held nothing.

Brian's parents and sister left immediately after the funeral and, as they said their goodbyes, she was sharply aware it was the last time she would see them. *No great loss,* she thought, wondering if they shed a tear—she supposed they did, but, such things were best left to privacy. Neither parent inquired about Brian's belongings and, when Colbie mentioned them, his mother instructed her to do with them as she pleased. And, that was that . . .

Colbie was alone with her grief.

Cassius Sprague ordered his caddy to pull a three iron as he calculated the distance to the hole. "What do you think? One eighty?"

The caddy plucked the club from the leather golf bag, calculating the length of the fairway. "Maybe more—two hundred, max." He stood beside his boss, taking into account he was talking to a man who didn't like to be wrong. "What do you think?"

Sprague was silent as he reassessed. "Two—give me the two . . ."

"I agree, Sir . . ." The caddy yanked the two iron from the bag, replacing the three at the same time. "Better to split the difference—one ninety, I'd say."

Taking his stance, Cassius Sprague wiggled his butt a few times in an effort to perfect his swing, then promptly shanked the ball into the pond. "Damn it!"

That was the first round of expletives.

The caddy didn't comment, fully aware if he opened his mouth, it may be his last day at work—and, on earth.

"I told you this was the wrong club," Sprague screamed, alerting everyone within a five-hole radius he wasn't to blame.

"Yes, Sir—my fault, Sir."

Sprague threw the two-iron at the caddy's feet, storming off toward his golf cart. Moments later, he peeled out—well, as much as one can peel out in a golf cart—heading for the clubhouse and a couple of shots, leaving the caddy to find his own way home.

When the bartender glanced at Sprague as he entered the clubhouse bar, he poured a Glenlivet, neat, asking the server to tell him it was on the house. Years ago, he learned who needed the extra stability of a stiff drink, especially after what most would consider a miserable showing on the links. A vital contributor to the cause, Sprague's money was always at the forefront of golf course administration's actions, and anyone dealing with the high rollers were instructed to make course patrons happy.

It was a plan that worked well and, as the bartender surmised would happen, after a few shots, Sprague's displeasure began to recede. Within the hour, his total score became more impressive as he tipped one or two with his buddies, each recounting their own successful rounds. But, by five o'clock, it was only Sprague and Buford Collins—a minor player in the pharmaceutical industry—left to tout their own worth.

There was small talk, of course, but, eventually, conversation turned to Mariska Clyburn's disappearance. "I suppose you know," Sprague mentioned, "Clyburn has an investigator poking around . . ."

Buford nodded, his pudgy, pickled-looking fingers clasping a rocks glass on the small table. "From what I hear, it's dead . . ."

Sprague's expression changed from gettin' drunk happy, to a targeted focus. "What does that mean? Mariska, or the investigation?"

"It means the investigator hasn't been seen for months."

"How do you know?"

Buford's eyes narrowed. "I just know . . ."

Sprague straightened in his chair. "Care to share?"

Collins thought for a moment, then took a sip of his drink. "I'm sure—if I were to discuss my thoughts—you'll certainly return the favor . . ."

"Of course . . ."

Again, Collins was silent, weighing his position with Cassius Sprague. 'Blackmail' had such an—ugly—ring to it, and he had to be careful how he presented what he knew. If Sprague demanded to know his sources?

Conversation over.

"So, the question becomes, Cassius, what's in it for me?"

Sprague didn't flinch—he expected it. "You know we're continuing Clyburn's research on cell degeneration—I think it's only fair you're kept apprised of our progress, don't you?"

Collins glanced out the window, then back at Sprague. "Plus?"

"I'm certain we can figure out something . . ."

Both waited, patiently giving the other time to consider the understood terms. Even though there would be no handshake, each knew the consequences of failing to follow through. "Indeed . . ."

Of course, Sprague had no intention of mentioning Bio-Com's halting Mariska Clyburn's research.

It was such an—inconsequential—detail.

Summer staked its claim, Savannah's temps soaring well above normal. A sticky heaviness lingered in the air as Colbie sat alone at a coffeehouse table, trying to review her last notes regarding Mariska Clyburn's disappearance.

Returning to work was something she didn't want to do—it would've been easier to lock herself away to deal with her grief for as long as she saw fit. But, in her gut, she knew Brian would consider such actions weak. After his passing, she retreated into her shadow world, seeking solace in the little bits of happy memories she allowed to surface. Staying there, however?

She couldn't allow it.

"Colbie?"

She turned, the voice familiar. "Holy crap! What are you doing here?"

Ryan burst into a huge grin. "What kind of greeting is that for an old friend?" He pulled her from her chair, his embrace warm and comforting.

She stepped back, holding him at arm's length. "I can't believe you're standing in front of me!"

He laughed, obviously delighted. "Where's Brian? The restroom? That guy never could hold his iced tea!"

Colbie's eyes filled with tears. "Don't you know?" A quick glance told her he didn't.

His eyes narrowed with concern. "Know what?"

She could barely speak the words. "Brian . . . Brian was killed in a plane crash a few months ago . . ."

The look on his face said everything as he pulled her to him again, wrapping his arms around her. "God . . . I'm so sorry . . ."

"I tried to get in touch with you, but your number wasn't the same . . ."

He blinked hard, refusing to allow his tears to spill into her hair. "I changed it after we put the Cape Town case to bed . . ."

And, there they stood, wrapped in grief, both not knowing what to say.

Perhaps there was nothing to be said.

Although she felt they shouldn't have, Colbie and Ryan spent the better part of the day together reminiscing about Brian, both hesitating to say goodbye at day's end—somehow, parting didn't seem right.

"I can really use a glass of wine," she confessed as he maneuvered his car against the curb in front of the inn. "Join me?"

Ryan turned slightly, leaning against the driver's door so he could see her better. It was a few years since they worked together on the case in Cape Town and, since then, they lost contact. Not because of intention—things just seemed to work out that way. But, as he sat with her beside him, he realized she would never be the carefree woman he once knew. Sadness haunted her eyes, her smiles only offered in obligation.

"Yep . . ."

Within ten, they sat in the comfortable front room of the inn, Colbie sipping a glass of merlot while Ryan opted for an ice-cold craft beer.

"So—what brings you to Savannah?" As she heard the words come out of her mouth, she realized their time together that day was filled with memories—he didn't offer why he was in Georgia, and she didn't ask.

"Work—after we parted in Cape Town, I took a little time to reorient myself."

"Reorient? What do you mean?"

"Oh, I don't know—you have to admit, there was a lot going on then. Brian. You. The possible breakup. It was just a lot . . ."

Colbie nodded. "I can't believe it's been so long . . ." She thought for a moment, then couldn't resist asking her next question. "What work?"

Ryan grinned, knowing she couldn't resist any sort of possible intrigue. "Corporate espionage . . ."

"Seriously?"

"Well, sort of—I'm just getting started, and I don't know crap about the pharmaceutical industry. Time to figure it out, though . . ."

Colbie choked a little on her wine. "Pharmaceutical? You've got to be kidding!"

"No—my client called me at the end of last week to investigate research theft. I got down here yesterday, and I was barely beginning my investigation when I ran into you."

She couldn't believe what she was hearing! "What's your client's name? If you're okay with divulging that information, that is . . ."

Ryan looked at her, his smile warm and familiar. "Okay—I guess . . ." He took a dramatic pause, a swig from his beer, then placed the long-neck bottle carefully on the side table beside his chair. "Bio-Com Pharmaceuticals—they specialize in R & D for the drug biz." He focused on her, his eyes narrowing—he knew that look. "Why?"

"Because . . . I'm on a case for the owner of Clyburn Pharmaceuticals! Monroe Clyburn—his daughter vanished last December, and hasn't been heard from since . . ."

They sat for a moment, both considering their individual cases. Finally, Ryan broke the silence. "This is weird—you and I connecting after so long, and we're working the same side of the fence? You gotta admit—that's stinkin' weird!"

For the first time in months, Colbie busted out her delightful, gut laugh. "Well, I can't argue that!"

"The question is what are we going to do about it?"

"What do you mean?"

"Well, it seems to me, we might be working on the same side . . ."

For the next three hours, they sat in the cozy, comfy parlor, discussing aspects of their individual cases, both realizing they might be able to help each other by joining forces. How, they weren't sure.

"Like old times," he commented as he stood, grabbing his keys. He looked at her for a moment, then held out his arms. Unable to resist the comfort of a good friend, she slipped into them easily, both quiet for a few moments. With a quick squeeze, Ryan was first to break the embrace. "I'll call you in the morning . . ."

She nodded. "We need to sit down to compare notes . . ."

With that, he was gone, leaving Colbie with a slight smile.

It really did feel like old times.

CHAPTER

8

onroe Clyburn sat across the table from his wife, an expensive Cuban cigar cradled in his fingers. Although he understood Colbie's taking a hiatus from the case, he wasn't one hundred percent convinced she was still right for the job. "Maybe," he confided to Agatha, "she's not as good as her reputation says she is . . ."

"Good heavens! Why on earth would you say that? The poor woman just lost the love of her life, and you're doubting her ability to do her job?"

It was a part of his personality she didn't like. He had the ability to write people off no matter the circumstances—

and, he made it clear to his wife he wasn't going to give her much time to come up with new discoveries in the case.

"She has until the end of the month—she had several months to show me something, and what do I have for my money?" He didn't wait for an answer as he roughly extinguished the cigar in a pricey ashtray. "I'll tell you what—nothing!"

Clyburn pushed away from the table. "I'm watching everything she does from here on out . . ."

With that, he left the room, leaving his wife to pick up the pieces of their cozy, supposedly romantic, dinner. Watching him go, she was unaware of her manicured nails impatiently tapping the tabletop.

Perhaps it's time, she thought. *Perhaps it's time . . ."*

By nine-thirty the following morning, Colbie and Ryan sat with cups of coffee in front of them, notes spread out on the small table in her room. To some, their location to meet might smack of impropriety, but she didn't care—they were discussing sensitive information that could be of interest to prying ears.

"So—you're working for Cassius Sprague?" She watched as Ryan clicked his pen, poised to take notes.

"Correct . . . and, Monroe Clyburn brought you on in the spring, right?"

"Exactly . . ."

"To find out what happened to his daughter . . ."

Colbie nodded. "Mariska—but, there's something strange about this case. For the months Brian and I worked on it, we didn't find out much . . ."

"Because?"

"I don't know—it's as if information were purposefully being kept from us."

Ryan looked up from his notes. "What's your gut?"

"That's just it—I don't have much of a gut. Nothing seems to make sense—but, I have a strong sense of everywhere I go is filled with lies. Deception . . ."

For the next several hours, they discussed their mutual cases and, by the time they called it quits? There was no doubt something rotten was afoot—not only with Monroe Clyburn's outfit, but with Cassius Sprague's, as well.

"I'm starving—a late lunch?" Ryan threw his pen on the table, then stretched his arms toward the ceiling.

Colbie was up like a shot. "Yes! I'm famished!"

A fifteen-minute walk led to a quaint restaurant in downtown Savannah, it's ambiance in keeping with the deep south. But, as Colbie entered the small, brick building, she suddenly shuddered.

"You can't be cold," Ryan commented as he held the door for her.

"No—but, I just felt a chill . . ." She stopped for a second. "It's nothing, I'm sure . . ."

A twenty-something hostess showed them to a table tucked in the corner—one which many considered the best in the house. But, on hot Savannah evenings, most patrons preferred the pleasantness of the patio—Colbie and Ryan, however, enjoyed the cool of air conditioning, their table's location providing unintended privacy.

As they waited for drinks, Colbie realized she knew nothing of Ryan's years since their case together in Cape Town. "So—you know pretty much everything that's happened in my life—now, it's your turn . . ."

He smiled, his response interrupted by their server. Both thanked her as she placed their drinks in front of them. "Can I get you anything else?"

They assured her she couldn't, returning to the conversation as she headed for the kitchen door. "Well?" Colbie waited for a response to her prompt.

"Well, after Cape Town . . ." He hesitated, unsure of how much he should say. "I returned home, and pretty much carried on as usual—I was fortunate in that cases seemed to drop in my lap, and I found myself busier than I ever thought possible."

"But, that's a good thing!"

"You're right—but, I still felt something was missing."

Her eyebrows arched. "Such as?"

"I felt as if I were—incomplete."

"So, how did you deal with that?"

Ryan shifted uncomfortably. "There was . . . someone."

Colbie didn't know what to say—but, unexpectedly and for some weird, inexplicable reason, his words stung. Still, as much as she wanted to, it wasn't her place to inquire. "I take it things didn't work out . . ."

Her old friend was quiet for a moment. "No—it didn't."

The signal to move on.

"Ready to eat?"

He laughed, thankful he didn't have to elaborate on his last three years. "Yep! What's good?"

"I haven't been here before, but you know how I love crab!" Instantly, she recalled saying the same thing to Brian shortly after they arrived in Savannah. For a fleeting moment, she wondered how she could feel so comfortable with Ryan not long after Brian's passing. Still, his friendship was obvious, and she welcomed the diversion from her grief.

A grief consuming her days.

She held his hand, palm up, tracing individual lines with her index finger. "Things are changing," she commented as he sat quietly, listening to every word. "And, you must be ready . . ."

He shifted uncomfortably. "Ready for what?"

She glanced at him, then gently pulled his hand closer so she could get a better look. After a moment she let go, then sat back in her chair. "It isn't clear—but, I sense you are in danger."

The man didn't flinch. "Danger? From what?"

"The question isn't from what—but, from whom . . ."

Still, the man sat motionless. "When?"

"Soon . . ."

Suddenly, he rose, tucking a hundred dollar bill in the small jar she always kept on the table. Without word, he strode from the room, the curtain separating the tiny room from the rest of her home catching slightly on his shirt. Impatiently, he batted it away, his mind filling with possibilities. Then, the door latched quietly as he stepped onto the street, thinking of what to do next.

At the window, she watched him go, curious about his thoughts. *Did he understand*, she wondered, as her perfectly manicured fingernails discreetly pulled back the edge of the curtain so she could view him as he climbed into a cab.

Perhaps.

"Good to have you back . . ." Kevin glanced at Colbie, noticing she wasn't the happy-go-lucky woman he met only a few months prior.

She didn't look at him. "Thank you—in a weird way, it feels good to be back . . ." It was strange, though—that morning she was sitting with Ryan instead of Brian, planning their cases.

"Where to?"

She checked her notes. I'd like to drop in on Melbourne Clyburn again—do you remember where he lives?"

Kevin grinned, then tapped the GPS on the dashboard. "We'll be there in about forty-five minutes . . ."

They rode in silence, Colbie not feeling like talking, and Kevin wondering what he could possibly say to slice the thick, uncomfortable air. Monroe Clyburn filled him in about Brian's death before he returned to chauffeuring her around the city, but he wasn't fully prepared to deal with someone who chose to stare out the window, saying little.

Within the estimated forty-five minutes, Kevin pulled onto the familiar street. "Something feels different," Colbie commented as he eased to a stop. Suddenly, she gripped his forearm. "Duck!"

Both scrunched down in their seats, Colbie stealing a glance at the man locking Melbourne's front door. Dressed in an impeccably tailored suit, he glanced at his shoes, then bent down to impatiently brush off whatever it was catching his eye.

"Stay down," she ordered as the man turned toward the street, glancing both ways.

Kevin remained still, his heart racing.

Holy shit! That's Melbourne! She peered above the dashboard as he pressed the key fob to his car which, until then, Colbie hadn't noticed. How she missed it, she didn't know—the sleek, expensively styled late model car was out of place on such a middle class street. But, it confirmed what Colbie already suspected—Melbourne Clyburn was a complicated man. A duplicitous man.

A curious man.

"So—that's it. I don't know who, and I don't know how—but, it's your job to figure it out." He stood. "If you have any questions, you know how to get in touch . . ."

Ryan rose, extending his hand. For the past two hours, he and Cassius Sprague spoke privately about what was transpiring at Bio-Com Pharmaceuticals. For several months, Sprague suspected confidential research data was finding it's way into the wrong hands—even so, he was unable to track the source. It was unconscionable any of his staff would stoop to something so low—so dangerous—but, if emails to his personal, private, account were true? Someone was planning to bring him down. Of course, the sender chose to remain anonymous and, at first, Sprague paid the information little mind—until Mariska Clyburn's name was dropped into the mix.

The thing was, none of it made any sense—the company's work was always protected, and anyone coming on board was pressured to sign a non-disclosure agreement. Up until then, there wasn't one person he could think of who didn't readily agree, without question. After all, the company was dedicated to cell regeneration research, something important to worldwide medical patients.

Unfortunately, Sprague's memory wasn't what it used to be, forgetting there were several in the employ of his company whom he overlooked their signing of the required document. To him, they were loyal researchers, bent on making their contributions to medicine.

"I will—give me a few days, and I'll get back with you about my findings . . ."

The men parted, each with his own expectation. But, there was one thing Ryan knew as he bade the receptionist a good afternoon—whatever he was about to uncover was linked to Colbie's case.

Time for a serious talk.

Although they hadn't planned to get together that evening, Colbie and Ryan relaxed on two lawn chairs in the inn's tiny backyard. It was private and, for what they needed to discuss, the fewer pairs of ears to listen, the better.

"I had a meeting with my client this afternoon," Ryan commented as he leaned back on the comfy chaise lounge.

"Sprague?" She, too, was ready to relax, but, unless they were in the privacy of her room, she kept a wary eye for someone lingering a little too long.

He nodded. "Although we spoke at length on the phone when he hired me, I wanted to meet him in person—you know, to get a feel for him."

"I know what you mean—so, are you at liberty to discuss your case?"

Ryan sat up, swinging his legs over the side of the chaise. "Haven't we already done that?" He paused. "That's what I want to talk to you about . . ."

Colbie straightened in her chair then focused on him, shading her eyes from the setting sun. "I don't get it . . ."

"Well—as I was talking to Sprague this afternoon, I got the feeling our cases are inextricably entwined . . ."

"And?"

He hesitated, wondering whether what he was about to suggest could possibly be misconstrued. After a few moments' thinking, he answered. "It makes sense if we join forces . . ."

"But, we did—or, do you mean work together as if it's one case?"

"Sort of—I think, if we work together, we can solve both cases. But, only we will know of our alliance . . ."

Colbie reached for the light sweater she grabbed when they decided on the privacy of the backyard. "Let me see if I understand you—we work together to solve both of our cases? I'm not sure how that's going to work . . ."

"It's simple—we share every bit of information we uncover . . ."

"But, as far as I can see, your case doesn't have anything to do with mine. Or, as least, I don't think it does—do you believe someone at Bio-Com is responsible for Mariska Clyburn's disappearance?"

Ryan shook his head. "Not yet—but, don't you think it's more than a little strange we were brought in as investigators within the same industry?"

"Well—yes. It's a little weird . . ."

"C'mon, Colbie! It's more than a little weird! I know from working with you, you're the first person to dispel coincidence . . ."

It was true. From the time Colbie realized she had a gift of what many termed 'second sight,' she always felt there was no such thing as coincidence.

"So—what do you have in mind?"

He looked at her, his expression serious. "We work together like we did in Cape Town . . ."

It was a suggestion Colbie didn't expect. The truth was she wasn't sure if working with Ryan would be disrespectful to Brian. Ryan and she had a brief, unspoken history, after all, one which neither could—or, wanted to—tuck under the covers.

"I don't know . . ."

"Look—I know what you're thinking—and, I also know you're thinking about Brian . . ."

Colbie nodded, her eyes filling with tears.

"I'm not saying we resurrect it—all I'm saying is we work together. That's it . . ."

She closed her eyes. For months, all she could see was the plane wreckage, its power eclipsing other information provided by her intuitive mind. Yes, she had twinges of visions, but she felt as if she were blocked, and she knew her contribution to Ryan's case would be nothing like their working together in Cape Town.

Without looking at him, she confessed. "I haven't experienced visions since Brian died . . ."

Ryan said nothing.

"I don't know if I still can . . ."

He stood, offering her his hand, pulling her up from her chair. "Oh, I have faith in you!"

"The problem is I don't know if I have faith in myself . . ."

CHAPTER

9

Marcus answered the door on the second, impatient ring, thoroughly exasperated he had to open it himself. *I pay a pretty penny for the best help money can buy—the least they can do is answer the damned door!* He yanked on the large, handcrafted handle, reminding himself to reprimand whomever was on staff.

"What the hell are you doing here?"

Melbourne delighted in his brother's instant discomfort the second he laid eyes on him. "Is that any way to greet your brother?"

Marcus hesitated, thinking for a moment his life would be much better if he slammed the door in Melbourne's face. Unfortunately, he could never make good on such desires simply because his loving brother would rat him out to his mom. That—would make life impossible.

He stepped aside, allowing Melbourne entry, skipping an offer to sit down, or enjoy a tall, cool glass of iced tea. "I'll ask again—what do you want?"

His brother's eyes grew cold. "We need to talk . . ."

"About?"

Melbourne cast a disgusted look, quickly scanning the room to make certain no one was around. "You know about what . . ."

Marcus met his gaze, refusing to let his usual wimp of a brother to control him. "There's nothing to discuss— nothing's changed."

"Perhaps—but, our dear mother dropped the bombshell about the investigator resuming her duties. I think it's prudent we make certain everything is in order. Don't you?"

"Like I said—nothing's changed."

The next thirty seconds?

A standoff.

Finally, Marcus opened the door, his signal clear. "If that's all . . ."

Melbourne didn't argue—he made his point. He shot a scathing glance at his brother as he crossed the threshold, promising himself to look into matters. "I'll be in touch . . ."

Marcus didn't bother watching him walk down the slate sidewalk. Instead, he slammed the door, intent on locating the poor, young woman who made the decision not to keep him shielded from unwanted guests.

In his mind, Buford Collins replayed his conversation with Cassius Sprague, privately devising the best plan to soak Sprague for as much as he could get.

It was the way he usually did business.

Sprague, however? A big fish. In Collins's mind, that made his situation much more precarious. Unlike his competitors, he wasn't quite at the level of having people do his bidding, and he usually had to do his dirty work himself. The good thing was he had sources—and, he never hesitated to use them, keeping each on his payroll by paying their fees with a favorite substance. It was a business tactic that made sense, the best part being the slugs he chose to deal with were cheap. For next to nothing, Collins could reign his fledgling pharmaceutical empire with an iron fist, accomplishing everything on his to-do list.

No longer would he be a minor player.

The question was were his sources enough to strike a blow aimed directly at Clyburn Pharmaceuticals? Perhaps it was a mistake to bring up the founder's missing daughter with Sprague, but he had a feeling Sprague harbored an underlying animosity toward Monroe Clyburn. If that were true . . . well, he wasn't sure, but, usually, his feelings were right on the money. This time? He had a feeling he was going to be rich . . .

He also had a feeling someone was watching him.

Someone close . . .

"Okay—let's go over everything we know about the two principal players . . ."

"Clyburn and Sprague . . ."

Colbie nodded. "I did a thorough background check on Monroe before I accepted the case, and there wasn't much pointing to nefarious activities . . ."

Ryan laughed, concentrating on his laptop. "Nefarious activities?"

"You've always been jealous of my vocabulary . . ." She smiled at him, then started flipping through her files.

Both slipped into a comfortable silence, each working on a plan to meld their cases. Although neither mentioned it, the atmosphere was lighter, somehow—it felt as if they'd been working together without a three-year hiatus.

"What's your schedule for tomorrow," Colbie finally asked, taking off her glasses.

"I'm just figuring that out . . . why?"

"Do you think you'll have time to do a little surveillance?"

"Maybe—who do you have in mind?"

She handed him a dossier on her client, Agatha's photo first in the file. "Agatha Elizabeth Clyburn—formerly Agatha Culpepper."

Ryan studied the picture for a moment. "Why?"

"I don't trust her as far as I can throw her . . ."

"Is that a well-thought out mistrust, or do you have a feeling about her?"

"Good question—it's more of a feeling. Since we started working together on this case, it seems my intuitive senses are returning."

"You had a vision about Agatha?"

"Yep—she was rushing to meet someone, although I couldn't get a handle on the location. While she was running, she turned, her face contorted with paralyzing fear . . ."

"So . . . someone was chasing her?"

"I think so—or, something. But, I didn't get a strong sense of who—or, what—it was."

Ryan thought for a moment, then focused on Colbie. "Well, the good news is your abilities seem to be returning!

And, in answer to your question, I'll tail Agatha tomorrow—
do you happen to know her schedule?"

"Oh, please—do I know her schedule? Of course, I do!"

For the remainder of the morning, research turned
to Agatha Clyburn, Colbie focusing on her early life with
Monroe while Ryan took the later years. Both quickly came
to the conclusion she was squeaky clean—except for that
one time in college.

The time she and Monroe had to answer to the court.

Colbie glanced at Ryan over her reading glasses. "Get a
load of this—I was fishing around public records from way
back, and it seems Agatha and Monroe got themselves in a
peck of trouble when they were seniors in college . . ."

"What kind of trouble?"

"Possible murder . . ." She waited for his reaction.

"Are you kidding?" He paused, thinking about the
indisputable fact Monroe and Agatha left college to live rich,
fruitful lives. "Possible? Clearly, they weren't responsible . . ."

"Apparently not—it was finally ruled an accident."
Colbie scrolled her computer screen down to read the rest of
the story. That piece of news certainly begged the question
about Monroe's and Agatha's possible propensity to be
involved in the sordid—things clearly below their station.
If nothing else, it was a toxic, little stain on their otherwise
perfect lives, and Colbie was certain there were more. "Did
you find anything after she married Monroe," she asked.

"Not much—pretty run of the mill, although she kept
out of the limelight. It seems both of them did . . ."

"That seems a little strange, don't you think? Although,

to be fair, she's quiet and reserved. Maybe society life doesn't suit her . . ." Colbie thought for a minute. "Tomorrow is a charity event—a luncheon, if I recall. Monroe mentioned, if I recall . . ."

"Did he make a point of telling you about the lunch?"

She shook her head. "No—it was really more within conversation. A charity benefiting cell degeneration research, I think. Why?"

"Well, if she doesn't like society functions, it seems strange she's going to this luncheon."

"You'd think . . . but, maybe she considers it her duty. Charity is, after all, a huge part of southern society. And, she's a society matriarch . . ."

"Maybe . . . anyway, I'll go to the function looking spiffy. If I go like this, they'll turn me away at the door!"

They laughed, Colbie eyeing his sweatpants, t-shirt, and running shoes. "No—they wouldn't do *that!*"

That moment was when things changed again for Colbie, and she began to feel a breath of freedom breeze through her body. For a moment, her grief laid down, allowing her the pleasure of enjoying—well, life.

CHAPTER

10

*T*hen, news. A body. Submerged in a rushing, swollen river outside of a small town north of Savannah. Of course, by that time, there was little left— dental records confirmed Mariska Clyburn's life terminated months earlier and, after examination of the remains, the coroner speculated she didn't die in the river—but, he really didn't know. Bits of decaying flesh clung stubbornly to their anchors, portions of her skull missing possibly due to blunt-force trauma.

The coroner couldn't be sure of that, either.

Colbie and Ryan learned of the discovery on the late night news, leaving Colbie to wonder why Monroe didn't contact her. "I imagine your case will come to a close," Ryan commented as she kept her eyes glued to the television.

But, she didn't hear. Completely still, the image in front of her wasn't from the television—it played out in her mind's eye. As she watched, a man—she couldn't tell who it was—stood with Monroe Clyburn, his face contorting with rage. Then, beside both of them, a hand rising from the ground, reaching and spreading it's fingers, one crooked index finger pointing at the unknown man.

Colbie turned to Ryan. "Mariska Clyburn's murder . . ." She paused, recalling the macabre vision. " . . . is the tip of the iceberg."

Ryan didn't look at her, continuing to watch the seasoned news anchor describe the scene by the river. "What iceberg?"

Colbie didn't answer right away, but only because she wasn't sure. "I don't know—all I know is Mariska Clyburn's murder wasn't because of industry espionage, or anything else related to why both of us are here."

Ryan sat up, turned down the volume, giving her his full attention. "Not espionage?" He thought for a moment, thinking about how her vision might impact his own case. "Then, that puts my situation in a different light, doesn't it?"

She nodded. "It's possible—all I know is the reason Mariska Clyburn was murdered didn't have anything to do with the original reason I accepted the case. She was targeted—by whom, I don't know . . ."

"So, nothing to do with cell degeneration, stealing secrets, or anything like that . . ."

"Nope—I wish it did. I also have a feeling Monroe Clyburn knows it . . ."

Both sat watching the silent television, thoughts private and unspoken.

Colbie's initial reaction proved correct—Clyburn fired her the day after Savannah's finest informed him his daughter's body was found. "There's nothing else," he told her, his voice stern and uncompromising.

Then, she asked him a question setting him back on his haunches. "Do you know who killed Mariska?"

Spittle spewed from his mouth, his knuckles whitening as he gripped the edge of his desk. "How dare you! Get out!"

Colbie stood, his reaction predictable. "I'm sorry. I didn't mean . . ."

Clyburn refused to show her the common courtesy of standing when she headed for the door. "I'll have your check delivered to the inn this afternoon. After today, you're on your own for lodging . . ."

Without a word, Colbie crossed through the door, then turned to face the man who so rudely dismissed her. "It makes me wonder . . ."

He took the bait. "Wonder what?"

"Why you don't want me to investigate who killed your daughter—and, why?"

No answer.

"Could it be," she continued, eyeing him slyly, "you know more than you care to tell?"

No comment.

Colbie transferred to Ryan's hotel that afternoon. He offered his room since it was a suite, but Colbie politely declined, feeling accepting his offer would be inappropriate.

They met for dinner in her room, tossing possibilities on the table as they came to mind. "There's one thing," Ryan commented, "we need to discuss . . ."

There was a seriousness in his voice she hadn't heard for a long while. "What's that?"

"Well . . . what do you say we make it official?"

She looked at him, her right eyebrow arching. "Official?"

"Yeah—I think it's a good idea!" He held her stare, knowing he was pulling her chain. "Don't you?"

"Well—what do you mean, 'official?'"

"Partners! We work well together, and . . . well, it just

works."

"Oh!"

"Well?"

She looked at him, wondering what Brian would say. "I don't know, Ryan . . ."

He pushed his plate away. "What's not to know—you know I'm right."

That was the thing—she did know.

By dessert, he convinced her, and a new alliance was formed, but only for their current case. Both were comfortable with each other, and it took about two seconds to get down to business. "I think we need to take a different approach," he suggested. "In fact, starting over completely sounds like a good idea . . ."

"Agreed. Our investigation is no longer about only Mariska—but, that doesn't mean we're changing players."

"You're probably right—so, who stays on our list, and who goes?"

Colbie thought for a minute, then flipped to a new page on her legal tablet. "I've always had a feeling about the Clyburn boys—there's something fishy going on there."

"In what way?"

"Well, the first time I met Melbourne, he was like timid mouse for most of our conversation."

"Most of it? I'm not sure I get it . . ."

"It was weird—it was like he morphed into another person right in front of me! His voice deepened, and his eyes looked—steely. That's when I started to look at him with a different perspective . . ."

"Anything else?"

"Not long ago, I wanted to interview Melbourne again, but, when I got there, I couldn't believe what I was seeing—the man who was a mouse left his house, locked the door, and stepped into a ritzy car—and, he looked like a million bucks . . ."

"You mean the way he was dressed?"

"That—and, what seemed to be an overall attitude."

"What do you mean?"

"Well, when I first met him, he looked like a sniveling, ratty, little man. But, when I watched him leave his home? He was dressed in a custom-tailored suit, complete with French cuffs and gold cufflinks . . ."

Ryan scratched a few notes, then looked at her expectantly. "Okay—who else?"

"Marcus Clyburn—Melbourne's brother. Polite, but aloof. He answered my questions, but I didn't learn much from him—he is, however, much different than his brother."

"In what way?"

"Marcus clearly likes money, and he seems to fit into the Clyburn mold better than Melbourne. Everything in his house was expensive—his taste in art was obvious, as was his preference for expensive furniture."

"Did you meet anyone else while you were there? A wife?"

"Yes—and, that was interesting. Marcus didn't bother

to introduce her, and I had to ask . . . Winnie. Winifred Elizabeth Clyburn."

"Do you think it's worth trying to get an interview with her outside of Marcus's influence?"

Colbie nodded. "I think that's a good idea—a woman-to-woman thing."

"Okay—since Clyburn severed his contract with you, I'm guessing it's not going to be easy. And, I'm also guessing you'll no longer have access to Marcus and Melbourne."

"I know . . ." She grinned at him as she got up to pour another cup of tea. "I think we should implement good old Cape Town surveillance techniques!"

For the next hour they hacked out the following day's schedule. Ryan was still investigating his case for Cassius Sprague, and he had his own list of suspects to interview. His heart, however, wasn't in it—he was much more interested in working with Colbie, and it didn't make sense to be investigating a case with her in addition to his own. So, together, they made the decision Ryan, too, would sever his contract with his client, leaving both of them free to begin a new investigation.

The problem was neither was clear on exactly what they were investigating.

Upon hearing of her daughter's passing, Agatha's wailing could be heard from the sidewalk for close to twenty-four hours. After that, an eerie silence dug in, and no one saw Monroe or Agatha until the memorial service nearly a week later. At the funeral, Agatha was clearly mourning, her face gaunt and pale with grief. Monroe, however, remained stolid through the entire service, refusing to give in to the pain in his heart and soul.

Colbie and Ryan watched from their SUV positioned across the street from the church. "It's been a long time since we were on surveillance together," he commented as he adjusted a small, inconspicuous pair of binos.

"I know—seems like old times, doesn't it?" She glanced at him, recalling their investigation in Cape Town.

He agreed, then fell silent as he watched those attending the funeral file solemnly from the church. There were few tears, and he and Colbie surmised everyone probably thought for months Mariska was a goner. Still, they had the good taste to go through the motions, greeting Clyburn and Agatha with a gentle handshake or hug.

"Check this out!" Ryan handed the binoculars to Colbie. "Who's that guy?"

She adjusted the lenses, focusing on a stocky, squatty, little man in an ill-fitting grey suit. "I don't know . . . why?"

"I'm not sure—it may be nothing, but, after he spoke briefly with Clyburn, he had a few words with my ex-client."

"Sprague?"

Ryan nodded. "And, they didn't look like friendly words."

Colbie continued to focus on the man neither she nor Ryan recognized, watching as he walked to his car, clicked the key fob, then climbed in a racy little number that didn't quite go with his clumsy-looking suit. "Take down these numbers . . ."

Moments later, the car sped away as if eager to get away from the maudlin scene. "Did you get them," Colbie asked.

"Yep—I'll run the plate in the morning . . ."

She looked at him, surprised. "That's not easy if you don't have contacts . . ."

He flashed his easy smile. "I don't recall saying I don't have contacts . . ."

"Buford Collins."

"Who the hell is Buford Collins?" Colbie didn't look up from her laptop. "The license plate?"

"Bingo! And, get this—he owns a small pharmaceutical

company, but isn't considered a major player."

Colbie cleared the monitor screen, then focused on Ryan. "Is that all you know?"

"Seriously?"

She laughed, admitting she knew better. "Okay—let me rephrase that—what else did you find out?"

He pretended to be slightly miffed. "Well . . ."

"Oh, for God's sake! Get on with it!"

He laughed, enjoying her response to his good-natured teasing. "Okay!" He waited a second before launching into everything he found out about Buford R. Collins. "Age fifty-seven. Height, five-nine . . ."

Colbie nodded. "Sounds about right . . ."

He founded Brightwood Pharmaceutical Company in nineteen eighty-seven . . ."

"Brightwood? Never heard of it . . ."

"Neither has anybody else, although there was a buyout attempt several years ago . . ."

"And?"

"Failed—it seems there was some dispute about the books, and the purchasing company rescinded its offer."

"Hmm—I wonder how Collins took that bit of news?"

Ryan shrugged. "Who knows—his company fell off the radar shortly thereafter."

Colbie thought for a few seconds. "Obviously, he knows Clyburn well enough to attend the funeral . . ."

"I thought of that—and, he can't be that much of an insignificant player if he's running in those circles."

"Anything else?"

He checked his notes. "Not really—he isn't married, and there doesn't seem to be anyone in his life. No pics of him online with anyone on his arm . . ."

Colbie recalled watching Collins walk to his car. There was something about him that struck her as—odd. And, when she thought of him at that moment, she was consumed with a feeling of overwhelming sorrow. "There's something about him," she muttered. "Something sad . . ."

"Why do you say that?"

"When I see him in my mind, I feel there's someone there—someone he can't see."

"What? You mean someone dead?"

"Maybe—I can't tell."

Ryan didn't say anything as he watched her work through what could only be a vision.

She glanced at him, sadness in her eyes. "I hear sobbing."

"Do you know who it is?"

Colbie shook her head. "No—all I know is it's someone close to Buford Collins. Nothing else . . ."

They sat quietly for several minutes, the air thick with something neither of them could explain. Finally, Ryan stretched his long legs. "I'm pooped . . ."

He hopped up, gave Colbie a kiss on top of her head, then headed to the door. "I'll call you at nine . . ."

Before she could respond, he was gone.

CHAPTER

11

*T*ime to act. "Kevin? It's Colbie—I hope you don't mind my calling you on your cell, but I remember you graciously offered your services, anytime . . ."

The voice on the other end laughed. "I take it this is one of those times?"

"Only if you're available—I absolutely don't want to create any problem at work . . ."

An uncomfortable silence. "Work? I guess you haven't heard—Clyburn canned me."

Colbie gasped. "What? Why?"

"That's just it—I'm not really sure. All he said was he didn't need me, anymore. And, that was it . . . I was done."

Colbie listened carefully, positive Kevin's termination had something to do with her. "When did he fire you?"

"A couple of days ago—all I did was ask him when you were picking up your investigation again, and he lost it!"

"What did he say?"

"About my firing?"

Colbie shook her head, although he couldn't see. "No—about me."

"Well . . ." Kevin hesitated, not wanting to hurt her feelings.

Immediately, she picked up on it. "It's okay—I can take it!"

A deep breath. "Clyburn said you don't know your ass from a hole in the ground, and all you did was waste his money . . ."

Colbie was silent for a moment. "Anything else?"

"No—but, every time I was driving you before . . ."

"Before I lost Brian?"

"Yes—he wanted to know everywhere we went, and everything we talked about. But, he wasn't interested in my part of the conversation . . ."

"Only mine?"

"Pretty much . . ."

Colbie considered Kevin's words carefully. "Well—it

seems you're out of a job because of me. So, what do you say to my hiring you to drive me as long as I'm in Savannah?"

"Seriously?"

She laughed. "Yes—seriously. But, I won't need you all the time—I'm working with a partner, and it may be I won't need you forty-hours a week. Are you okay with a part-time arrangement?"

Kevin quickly agreed and, after hashing out the particulars, they agreed to meet the following day. "And, I'll make arrangements for a rental car—I don't want you using your personal vehicle for work . . ."

Of course, there was more than one reason for that—if things got dicey, she didn't want Kevin anywhere near the line of fire. Tracing a license plate number?

Not that tricky.

Colbie and Ryan met for a quick bite around noon, then rehashed their afternoon appointments. She filled him in on her conversation with Kevin, both agreeing hiring him was the right thing to do, especially since he was fired because of her. It also made Ryan feel a little better—although Colbie could take care of herself, having Kevin around was a good thing.

"You know what I just figured out," she asked as she sipped her iced tea.

"What's that?"

She paused, gathering her thoughts, making sure they made sense. "I don't know if I mentioned it, but, Brian and I always felt we weren't making any progress on our case, and neither of us could figure out why . . ."

"Now?"

She leveled a serious look, putting down her glass. "I think Monroe Clyburn knew all along we wouldn't find anything—he knew Mariska was dead. Or, felt she was . . ."

"A wild goose chase?"

She nodded, new lines creasing her forehead. "Maybe. But, why? It doesn't make any sense—why would a client purposely put me on the wrong path?"

Ryan sat back in his chair. "Let me see if I'm getting it— you think Clyburn brought you in on the case, but, all along, it was a sham. Is that right?"

"Yes . . ."

"You think you were being intentionally deceived?"

"Hell, yes! I've been on this case—in one way or another—for months! And, I don't have jack shit! This case has been filled with the chill of deception since I got here . . ."

Both were quiet until Ryan drained his tea glass with dramatic flair—slurping.

Colbie looked at him with the appropriate amount
of disdain, then burst out laughing. "Did you manage—
somewhere along the line—to grow up?"

He slurped one last time. "Nope . . ."

It was interesting how much Colbie's life changed in
such a short time. After Brian's passing, Tammy—the best
assistant in the world—decided to move on after years
of working with them. Colbie was certain their change in
circumstances had something to do with it and, if she were
honest, she didn't blame her. After all, she was rarely in the
office and, although there was always something brewing
from an admin standpoint, it had to be a little lonely.

Now? Everything was up to her. She had a lot to
accomplish, and she had no intention of hiring anyone
without extensive background checks, interviews, and
anything else she could think of to help her determine who
would be perfect for the position. Even so, as of the time
she and Ryan split with their Savannah clients, no one was
standing in line to snag the opportunity of a lifetime.

Tammy's departure? Another signal Colbie's life was in
transition.

Kevin picked her up just as Colbie was hanging up with Ryan, agreeing to meet for a late-afternoon lunch. "Hey, you!" Colbie hopped in the passenger's seat, then buckled up. "It's been awhile!"

He agreed. "I appreciate the job!"

Then, it was down to work. By noon, Colbie figured out there was a lot more to Kevin than anyone might suspect. Quiet and unassuming, he could easily give someone the impression of disinterest. But, she quickly determined that wasn't the case. It was clear—when she was investigating for Clyburn—her time with Kevin wasn't indicative of who he was, nor his innate capabilities.

After a quick run at the drive through, they munched on takeout as they figured out their next interview. "I don't think I want to interview anyone," Colbie commented as she unwrapped her sandwich. "Something tells me I need to be watching . . ."

Kevin glanced at her. "Watching what?"

"Not what—who. Buford Collins . . ."

He processed the name for a moment. "Never heard of him . . ."

"Neither had I until Ryan and I attended Clyburn's daughter's funeral . . ."

"Holy shit! You were there?"

"Well, kind of—we were across the street."

"So—who is he?"

Colbie hesitated, wondering if she were providing too much information. But, she supposed it didn't make any difference—Kevin was working for her and, even if Clyburn got wind of it, she didn't care. "He's in the pharmaceutical biz . . ."

"Okay—what can I do?"

A question catching Colbie off guard. "You mean in addition to driving?"

He nodded. "Yeah—I mean, I might be able to lend a hand . . ."

She looked at him, putting her intuition into action. From what she saw in three or four images in her mind's eye, she knew she could trust him. "You know what? You just might be right! Let's get through today, then we can chat about what you can bring to the table . . ."

Colbie never saw such a huge smile.

Ryan arrived at the venue shortly after eleven, a good thirty minutes before charity guests were slated to arrive. Doing so allowed him to people watch, his radar tuning to anyone who might make an unintended slip of the tongue, or a gesture intended only for certain eyes.

Backed up to a marble pillar in the historical hotel, he blended in with the decor—something he planned. As a seasoned private investigator, after his first case he realized the benefits of anonymity, and it was a technique Colbie taught him. Since then, he made it a point to check out locations so he would know what to wear.

Tucked out of sight, he watched as—promptly at eleven-thirty—guests began to arrive, social status on parade as they claimed chairs according to name cards strategically placed on beautifully decorated white round tables. Keeping supercilious chatter to respectful whispers, Savannah's finest socialites were fully aware of who was watching—and, who was not. Eyes inconspicuously scanned the room, taking names, deciding who they would grace with inconsequential conversation.

Arriving just shy of the limit of southern manners, Agatha Clyburn entered, everyone turning in her direction, then quickly averting their gazes—it would, of course, be rude to stare. Acknowledging the passing of a loved one is always difficult, especially in social settings, but . . . murder? Everyone knew that's exactly what it was, most considering it prudent to keep their gossiping mouths shut—it was easier to keep track from the fringes.

Ryan smiled, watching society mavens talk quietly until it was time for the event to begin. Agatha wore Mariska's death on her face, the challenges of the last several months digging in deeper as new lines took root. Then, as he was taking stock of the who's who in Savannah society, Agatha suddenly looked up at a woman standing next to her chair, momentary shock flitting across her face.

Stunned recognition.

"Stay back . . ." Colbie glanced at Kevin, then back at the man climbing into a late model sedan. "That's him . . ."

Kevin obeyed, staying within several car lengths once Buford Collins turned onto the highway, heading south. Thirty minutes later, he exited, then turned left on a country lane not far from the main road. "It's weird how quickly we can be in the country," Colbie commented as she kept an eye on Collins's car. "And, not only that—what the hell is he doing all the way out here?"

"Beats me—this is in the middle of nowhere! I haven't been here before . . ."

"Unfortunately," she observed as she scanned the area, "there's hardly anyone around—that makes us sitting ducks." She glanced at him. "I'm betting we won't be welcomed with open arms."

He nodded, his hands gripping the wheel. "It feels like a dirty, little secret back here . . ."

Colbie shot him a glance, his words capturing exactly how she felt. "I know what you mean . . ."

They followed Collins for another mile, until Colbie called it quits. "I don't have a good feeling about this—turn around."

"What?"

"Turn around!"

She didn't have to tell him again—Kevin swung the car around in a small clearing, heading back to the highway. But, just before pulling onto the main road, Colbie felt what could only be described as icy fingers gripping her neck.

She swiped at something she couldn't see.

"What? What's wrong?" Kevin slowed, keeping his focus on her more than the road.

She sat for a moment, then turned her attention to an overgrown thicket lining the lane, unsure of what she was feeling. "I don't know—I felt something . . ."

Then, she saw it.

A woman's face, darkly veiled in shadows of tangled branches and limbs, eyes black as ink.

The socialite bent down to kiss Agatha's cheek—probably from obligation, Ryan surmised, but, to most, it seemed a magnanimous gesture. Then? A strange thing happened. Agatha rose elegantly, touched the woman on her arm, spoke a few words, then headed for the double doors in the back of the room. *A hasty retreat,* he asked himself as he peered from behind the pillar.

It seemed so. The woman he didn't recognize appeared slightly out of sorts, her face set like stone as she greeted those at her table located directly in front of the dais. No one noticed as she quickly glanced toward the doors, but Ryan thought he noticed a look of superior satisfaction.

Five minutes later, he was out the door.

Agatha?

Nowhere to be found.

"Did you see that?" Colbie twisted her head, trying to keep her eyes on the woman.

"See what?"

She faced forward again, not certain she should say. "That woman . . ."

Kevin glanced at her, then back at the road. "I didn't see anyone . . ."

As they headed back to Savannah, Colbie thought about Collins. The woman. The country lane. It was more than a little disturbing when she made the decision not to follow his car—why, she couldn't explain. All she knew was there was a darkness she was ill-prepared to meet.

Kevin interrupted her thoughts. "Where to now?"

"You know . . . I think I'm ready to call it a day. Let's head back to the hotel, and you can pick up your car."

"Sounds like a plan!" Although Kevin didn't know Colbie well, he knew her well enough to know she was grappling with something—and, he suspected it had something to do with the face she saw in the thicket. "What about tomorrow?"

She thought for a moment, then dug in her messenger bag for a pen and scrap of paper. "Just a sec . . ." She scribbled something, then turned her focus to the calendar on her cell. "I'm not sure yet—how about if I call you in the morning?" She didn't like being so unsure of her schedule, but she needed to talk to Ryan before making plans.

Kevin grinned, as he pulled into the parking garage of the hotel. "Sounds good to me!"

"What's that supposed to mean?"

"Just what I said—I was followed . . ."

"To here?"

Collins sighed, taking a swig from a much-needed scotch.

"Did you listen to anything I said?" The second the words left his mouth, he knew he made a mistake—a big mistake.

"Excuse me?"

He refused to shrivel, although what he really wanted to do was drink himself into a non-forgiving stupor. "Forget it—I didn't mean it the way it sounded. I'm just frustrated, that's all . . ."

"About?"

He tried to keep his voice civil. "The car—the one that followed me when I turned off the main highway . . ."

"Maybe they took a wrong turn—you know it's easy to get lost out here. Besides, it's pretty clear they didn't follow you all the way." Beulah Brightwood stared at him with a modicum of disgust. "You worry too much . . ."

Buford drained his glass. "Yeah, well—if someone comes knocking, I don't want it to be a surprise . . ."

Several bracelets jangled slightly as she poured him another drink. "So—what are you doing to do?"

He looked up at her as she handed him a fresh glass. "I don't know—but, what I'm not going to do is hang around and do nothing!"

CHAPTER

12

*E*venings were what she missed most—she and Brian always debriefed at the end of the day, and it was a great way to connect. *Those days are gone forever,* she thought, slipping her feet into her slippers.

Time became of little consequence, and Colbie moved through her days—often with false bravado—only because it was expected. Ryan seldom brought Brian into their conversations, and she wasn't sure if that were because it was an uncomfortable topic, or consideration for her still-raw emotions. Either way, it left her to grapple with her grief alone and, so far, she wasn't winning.

Knowing what she did about human behavior and its accompanying frailties, she considered seeking professional help—but, only for a second or two. Her true refuge was the comfort she sought in the solace of her shadow world, and it was there she preferred to live the lonely moments of her life.

By the end of the evening, she felt as if every wound reopened, mocking her inability to get a grip. Ryan left nearly an hour prior, and she looked forward to connecting with her intuitive self. Did she hope Brian might make an appearance?

Of course.

That night? It wasn't meant to be . . .

"Where are you headed?" Colbie focused on the front doors of the hotel, trying to get a glimpse of Kevin.

Ryan looked at her, puzzled by the question. They hashed out their schedules the evening before, but, if he were honest, he thought she seemed a little off. Quickly, he decided that little detail wasn't worth mentioning.

"I'm heading toward the Clyburn's—it was too weird when Agatha left the charity gig, and I have a feeling she knows more than she's letting on . . ."

"About?"

"That's just it—I don't know, but, in some way, she's involved. I guarantee you that . . ."

Colbie agreed, then caught sight of Kevin. "He's here— I'll see you this afternoon . . ."

Ryan watched her rush through the revolving door, then climb into the rental car. *Something's not right,* he thought as the car pulled away from the curb. *Nope. Not right, at all . . .*

Agatha Clyburn stood in her kitchen, a fine china cup and saucer in her hands as she gazed through the window, her sorrow palpable—the woman's words sliced her soul, knowing the targeted effect of her comment, never considering showing up at the charity event was an ill-advised mistake.

She didn't mention it to Monroe—if he got wind of it? *There's no telling what he'd do,* she thought as she stared. *Besides, she's a nobody . . .*

Agatha didn't want to create a scene either at the charity function, or at home—her life's credo was 'let sleeping dogs lie,' no matter the situation. There was no sense in calling adverse attention to themselves—they were in the limelight too much already for her refined taste.

It was during those private moments she thought about her daughter. Early years of motherhood proved stressful for the young woman who was used to the finer things. Unknown to her husband—or, anyone—there were many tears shed in the bathroom, unsure if she were cut out for such things. There was no turning back, of course, but Agatha Clyburn yearned for a life unencumbered.

After Mariska's birth, she yearned for a life.

Boys, it turned out, were infinitely more manageable than girls. In fact, when she found out she was with her third child? Well, let's just say she wasn't thrilled. So, when Mariska was old enough to enjoy some sort of private schooling, Agatha shipped her off, unaware of the psychological damage she was heaping on her daughter.

The bold truth—albeit a private one—is Agatha Culpepper Clyburn was a cold, guarded, unemotional woman. According to some, she regarded her charity duties as obligations, not giving a hoot about the reason for the organization. She preferred privacy in all facets of her life, but Monroe insisted she be somewhat visible in the Savannah community. Once nominated for a well-established charity board position, she wanted to tell them to cram it—but, she politely declined, adding it would take too much of her time, the children being her priority.

As Mariska grew, tensions increased and, by the time Agatha's daughter reached her teens, communication was non-existent. It was a family secret not leaving the walls of their home, and Mariska's friends had no idea of their friend's dysfunctional situation.

"What are you doing?"

Agatha didn't move at the sound of her husband's voice. "Nothing—just enjoying a cup of tea."

Monroe grunted, throwing his suit jacket over the back of a kitchen chair. "You usually don't have tea . . ."

She continued staring out the window. "Perhaps, I'm changing . . ."

"What the hell does that mean?"

"Nothing—nothing, at all." She paused. "So—what's new at the pill factory?"

He launched a scathing glance. "The pill factory? My—aren't we feeling caustic today . . ."

"I meant no offense . . ." Her spidey sense cued her it wasn't a good time to be flippant. "I was just thinking about Mariska . . ." She put the cup and saucer on the counter, then sat next to him, slipping her hand over his. "I miss her . . ."

At that moment, it was too bad for Agatha her husband didn't feel like comforting his wife, indulging in what he considered worthless sentiment "She's gone, Agatha—we have to move on."

"I know . . ."

A thick silence.

He glanced at the stove. "What's for breakfast?"

"You want to go back?"

Colbie nodded. "There's something about it that gives me the creeps . . ."

As Kevin pulled away from the curb, he noticed her glancing back at the hotel. "Isn't that reason enough *not* to?"

She shot him a good-natured smile. "Not for me!"

Her driver laughed, delighted their relationship was becoming comfortable. "What does Ryan have going on today?"

"Other than keeping an eye on Agatha Clyburn, I'm not sure . . ."

"Ah—the lovely Agatha. She's quite a piece of work . . ."

She glanced at him, slightly surprised by his comment. "Do you know her?"

"Not really—I talked to her a couple of times, but nothing more than that."

"Then, why the 'piece of work' comment?"

"Well . . ." He looked left, then right before entering traffic. "Because I heard a conversation between Mariska and her at an employee Christmas party."

"When was that?"

"A couple of years ago—the Christmas before she disappeared, I think . . ."

"And?"

"Well—it was a little weird. Neither one of them knew I was there, and it was quite the heated argument . . ."

"At a Christmas party—that's strange."

"That's what I thought . . ."

"What were they talking about?"

Kevin glanced at her. "It wasn't about what to buy Daddy for Christmas, I can tell you that . . ."

"Explain . . ."

"When I stepped onto the veranda at the hotel where the company party was in full swing, I heard Agatha tell Mariska she was a snot-nosed little bitch for not appreciating the finer things in life . . ."

Colbie's eyebrows peaked. "Really?"

"Indeed—and, Mariska was having none of it. I couldn't hear what she said, but a few moments later she left her mother standing on the veranda by herself—well, and me, of course, only they didn't know it . . ."

"Was that it?"

"No—call me nosy, but I decided to keep an eye on them throughout the evening, and there was a decided frost between them."

"Did you catch wind of more conversation?"

"Indeed, I did! Agatha approached Mariska a couple of times, but she was having none of it—finally, Agatha gave up."

"What about the conversation?"

Kevin turned onto the main highway toward the country road where they followed Buford Collins. "It wasn't between Mariska and her mom—it was between Agatha and Monroe."

"What did they say?"

"She told him—what she thought was under her breath, and it would have been, too, had she not been half shit-faced—anyway, she told him she regretted having children and, as far as she was concerned, she could care less about any of them."

Colbie was quiet for several moments, considering Ryan's comment from earlier that morning. "Ryan told me he thinks Agatha is up to her eyeballs in something, but he's not sure what it is . . ."

Kevin nodded. "Agreed—I always had a weird feeling the few times I was around her, and it was one I didn't like."

It was at that moment Colbie knew the man sitting beside her wasn't only an intuitive, but part of her business— and, she had no doubt Ryan would approve. Kevin's being similar to her was a conversation for another time, however.

Just as Kevin was about to comment, they arrived at the small country lane thirty miles outside of Savannah. Overgrown thickets obscured any hope of getting a glimpse of where Buford Collins was headed the previous day, but Colbie refused to let her intuitive discomfort dissuade her from exploring.

"I don't see no trespassing signs . . ." Colbie kept her eyes glued to the narrow, dirt lane.

"Neither do I . . ."

After winding nearly a quarter mile into thick woods, trees opened to a lush, green clearing. A small cottage stood tucked into towering pines, its front porch small and welcoming.

"What now?" Kevin slowed to a stop before fully entering the clearing.

"Follow my lead—get out, and stand by the car as if you don't have a clue as to where you are . . ."

"Good thing I took acting in college . . ."

Colbie grinned, then hopped out, closing the car door quietly. Seconds later she was walking a gravel path to the porch when the front door opened. "Can I help you," a voice asked as Colbie stepped toward the door.

"I hope so—I was supposed to meet the real estate agent here, but I think I took a wrong turn . . ." She waited. No response. "I was here with my friend last evening to see if we could find it, but . . ." She turned, calling to Kevin. "What's the address?"

Kevin pulled a piece of paper from his pocket, glancing at it. "Seventeen thirty-five Magnolia . . ."

Suddenly, the woman stepped onto the porch. "Lane or Road?"

"Lane, or road," Colbie called to her driver.

"Road!"

The woman looked at Colbie with a smile. "This is Magnolia Lane . . ."

"Oh, no! I'm so sorry!"

The woman smiled again, then opened the screened front door. "No problem . . . good luck!"

It was a dismissive cue, to be sure, but Colbie wasn't about to let the woman go so easy. "This is breathtaking! It's stunning—so tranquil, and private . . ."

The woman closed the screen door before crossing the threshold. "It's been in our family for years—my grandfather built it when he first landed in Savannah."

Colbie glanced at her, taking in everything—her hair. Clothes. Approximate age. "When was that?"

"Oh, my land! Early thirties, if I recall correctly . . ."

Colbie scanned the property, making mental notes of size, buildings, and everything else within her sight. "Have you lived here long?"

"Long enough—when he died, the land and house fell to my sister. Then it came to me when she passed—that was about forty years ago."

"Oh . . ." It was an awkward moment, one which Colbie didn't want to sustain. She extended her hand. "Alexandra Polson—everyone calls me Alex."" She pointed at Kevin. "That's Robby . . ." She waved, and Kevin played his part to the hilt, waving and smiling. "He's my brother's friend who said he knew right where Magnolia Road was . . ." She grinned. "Guess that's the last time I'm listening to him!"

The stocky woman laughed. "It's hot—would you like to come in for a glass of iced tea?"

"Really? I'd—we'd—love to!" Colbie turned, immediately signaling Kevin, hoping he'd play along.

When he reached the porch, Colbie took the lead. "This is Robby Benson—my brother's friend who doesn't know where Magnolia Road is!"

Kevin offered his hand. "Ma'am . . ."

"I know it's easy to get lost around here—I'm Beulah Brightwood. Please, come in . . ."

She graciously held the door for them as they stepped into a tiny foyer that opened into a deceivingly spacious living area to the right, kitchen to the left. "It's small, but it's home," she commented as they made themselves comfortable in two, over-stuffed chairs. "I hope sweet tea is alright—it's the way of the south . . ."

Colbie and Kevin assured her it was as both took note of Beulah's belongings. A small, round table held twenty or more framed pictures, most of two teenage girls enjoying life. No one who could pass for a husband or brother—only the two teens.

Carrying a tray with cookies and iced tea, Beulah joined them. "I hope your tea isn't too sweet . . ."

Colbie handed a glass to Kevin who clearly understood he was there only as a prop. "I couldn't help noticing the pictures on the table—is the dark-haired girl you?"

"Oh, yes—and, my sister, Gracie. She's the one I was telling you about. She passed many years ago . . ."

"I'm sorry—I can well imagine it's a pain that never goes away . . ."

"It doesn't . . ."

Colbie pretended she suddenly remembered something. "Brightwood . . . where have I heard that name?"

Beulah laughed. "Well, it could be because my step-brother owns Brightwood Pharmaceuticals. Maybe that's where you heard it . . ."

A good time to play dumb. "Maybe—that doesn't sound familiar, though." Then, she looked at Kevin. "You're from Savannah—have you heard the name, Brightwood?" Colbie timed her question perfectly—Kevin was munching on a cookie, and had his mouth full. He simply shook his head, then Colbie reclaimed the lead. "Well—it's not important. Your sister was young when she passed . . ." She hoped their hostess would take the bait.

She did. "Twenty-two—she died shortly before her college graduation."

"Again, I'm sorry—was she ill?"

Colbie took a sip of tea, trying to look innocent, with the perfect amount of silence prompting Beulah to continue.

"She was . . . well, I think she was murdered, but, at the time, no one else did."

Colbie focused on her. "Why did they think that?"

"All they said was there was no evidence of foul play, and they dropped it. An accident, they said . . ."

"Could it have been an accident?"

Beulah sighed, the pain of losing her sister on her face. "I suppose—but, it just doesn't feel right."

For the next hour, Colbie and Kevin learned about Gracie Brightwood, and how she was found lying face up on the bank of a swollen river. Three weeks later? Forgotten. Chalked up to an accident.

Case closed.

CHAPTER

13

*S*he said nothing, studying the cards in front of her for several minutes. Lightly, she brushed her fingertips over the card causing her the most concern. "The World. Big changes . . ."

"What kind of changes?"

She looked at him, knowing he knew what she was talking about, but, for some reason, he chose not to acknowledge. She pointed to the last card in the spread. "The Tower, coupled with the Six of Swords . . ." She paused, then turned her attention to her client. "Destruction . . ."

He said nothing, his face expressionless as he absorbed the seer's words.

"Your tower of lies is about to crumble . . ."

"When?"

"Soon . . ."

"What else?"

For the next thirty minutes, the Tarot card reader for the social elite shed light on his near future, as well as the possible, long-term outcome of his actions. As the man sat, listening, there was no denial—nothing to make one believe he couldn't be a part of such things. Did he believe her? Without doubt. "Can I change it?"

And, there it was. The question most asked when clients realize they stand at a choke point. "Perhaps . . ."

He glanced again at the cards, then at her. "How?"

Her eyes locked with his, her stare searing. "It means," she replied with clipped precision, "you must set your course. Should you choose to realign your life with something more productive, you can—but, it may be an exercise in futility should you not be fully committed . . ."

He held her gaze, undaunted. "Last time, you said I was in danger . . ."

"That is true . . ."

"Still?"

"Yes . . ."

He was quiet, her words jockeying for position in his brain. He figured there was no way she would possibly discuss his sessions with other clients, but, it wasn't out of range. Her client base was broad, and, hopefully, she knew it wouldn't be wise to compromise the most sacrosanct confessions—his, or the grotesquely elite. No—biting the hands that feed her didn't seem the best move.

"Tell me . . ."

She closed her eyes, silently tuning into the man sitting across from her. From previous readings, she anticipated his being guarded, but, that particular day? Impenetrable. Still, although it took her a little longer than usual, images began to swirl in and out of her mind's eye. "The one who seeks you will not stop until she finds out what she needs to know . . ."

"She?"

"Yes—and, one other."

"Male or female?"

"It is unclear . . ."

"Do I know them?"

"No . . . but, the woman? She is strong . . ." She hesitated, her eyelids fluttering as she interpreted image after image. "And . . ." Again, she paused. "She is like me . . ."

"Like you? I don't understand . . ."

The seer nodded, a knowing smile on her lips. "She sees beyond your world, as do I . . ."

"You mean she's psychic?" He waited for her response, the first signal of panic clutching his stomach, squeezing hard.

"Oh, yes—and, more. She understands . . ."

A surge of vomit rose in his throat.

Opening her eyes, she leaned forward with defined

urgency. "Oh, yes—you are, indeed, in danger . . ."

"I got an interesting call today . . ." Ernest Beddington reached for a slice of skillet cornbread, slathered soft butter on the top, then drizzled honey over every inch.

"Interesting how?" His wife watched, wondering how he stayed as thin as a rail.

"Well—I'm not really sure. No name, but a stark warning things might change quickly . . ."

"What? What things? Do you know who it was?"

Beddington recognized the alarm in her voice, a reaction he expected. Ever since they met and married decades ago, Mary Ellen wasn't the 'stiff upper lip' type—she preferred confiding and sharing the most intimate details of her life, convincing all who listened she was more suited to teas and bonbons.

It was a perk of educational station.

Her last question was the most important. "No," her husband replied. "I have no idea who it was. But, he did mention a name . . ."

"He?" She reached for the jam. "What name?"

"Clyburn. Monroe Clyburn . . ."

Mary Ellen stopped, bread and butter knife perched precariously over her cornbread, strawberry lusciousness inching closer to its sides. "The same Clyburns from Savannah?"

"That's my guess . . ."

She stared at him, trying to figure why anyone would be calling him about Savannah's social elite. "What does Monroe Clyburn have to do with you?"

Ernest crammed the last of the cornbread into his mouth. "That's just it—I don't even know the guy."

Mary Ellen thought for a moment. "He attended the university, didn't he? It seems I remember something about that—Joy Brooks mentioned his wife's name . . . Agatha, I think."

"What about her?"

"Oh, you know—eight women gossiping about anything and everything? I hardly remember what came out of my own mouth, let alone someone else's—besides, that was a long time ago."

"How long?"

"Months—six, at least."

They sat, both eying the last slice in the skillet. "Split it," he asked, knowing she would decline politely.

"No—you go ahead . . ."

More butter. More honey. "Do you know her?"

"Agatha? Good heavens, no—she's a little out of my league, don't you think?"

Ernest reached across the table, clasping her hand. "Don't sell yourself short, my dear—the Clyburns have nothing on you . . ."

Giving his hand a quick squeeze, Mary Ellen smiled.

She knew he was right.

Ryan listened as Colbie recounted her visit with Beulah Brightwood, both agreeing the Brightwood surname was, most likely, more than coincidence.

Colbie took off her reading glasses, then laid them on the table. "Nothing makes sense, though . . . what does Buford Collins have to do with Beulah? He doesn't seem the type to visit a cloistered cottage in the middle of nowhere . . ."

"Oh, I don't know—from the little we know about him, it's hard to tell. Maybe he and Beulah are friends . . ."

Colbie nodded. "You're right . . ."

"Of course, I'm right . . ."

"My—aren't we smug!"

"It's a skill I acquired over the last couple of years . . ."

She glanced at him, thinking of their relationship. She couldn't have asked for a better friend when things with Brian derailed a few years back. "It seems I missed a lot during that time . . ."

Silence.

Ryan's eyes met hers. "Maybe you did . . ."

"Maybe we both did . . ."

A tiny sliver of sorrow crept into their conversation, neither knowing what to say. Finally, Ryan brought things around to a mutual comfort level. "I think we're missing a key piece of information—and, I think it's right in front of us."

"If that's the case, let's go through it . . ."

"Agreed—let's start with what we know about Buford Collins. Which isn't much . . ."

"Exactly—I researched Brightwood Pharmaceuticals when the name cropped up, but, other than the failed buyout, nothing seemed out of the ordinary."

"Still—your interest was piqued enough to follow him to Beulah's. The question is why . . ."

Colbie thought for a moment, recalling her intuitive feeling when Collins first landed on their radar. There was something about him reminding her of a demon troll— squatty, his round belly the recipient of one too many beers.

She propped up her feet on the coffee table. "I remember thinking he appeared completely different than the upper crust attending Mariska's funeral . . ."

Ryan nodded. "I know what you mean—he didn't seem to be the type they'd hang out with . . ."

Another silence. "Tomorrow," Colbie finally continued, "we do a full-blown research on Mr. Buford Collins. I want to know everything about him—where he grew up, college, married . . . everything!"

"Me, or you?"

"Both of us—like we always did. You go one way, I'll go the other . . ."

"Check. Meet back here?"

"Yep—five-thirty?"

"Works for me!"

Colbie scrunched up her pillow to support her neck, then laid back and closed her eyes—it had been a long time since she connected with her intuition. Yes, impressions were always zipping in and out, but, since Brian died, she hadn't really taken the time—or, made the effort—to hone in on her current project. It was an element of a normal investigation she realized was missing, so, after kicking Ryan out of her hotel room earlier than usual, she eagerly anticipated the calm of meditation.

Her intuitive connection didn't take long. Soon after a customary affirmation, visions and images appeared, but they didn't disappear quickly, as usual—one-by-one they lingered, as if encouraging her to delve deeper into each to aid in deciphering its meaning.

As one vision faded, another blossomed into a series of images, as if she were watching a movie. Two figures—people—cloaked in black stood watching something below them, neither moving—whether they were male or female, she couldn't tell.

Her eyelids fluttered as she watched, scanning the area in her vision for recognizable landmarks. She knew the two figures were outdoors, but there was nothing to give her a clue about where they were, or why they were there. All Colbie knew?

It wasn't good.

Then, the image of a hand with perfectly manicured fingernails, its index finger pointing to the two figures. Immediately, Colbie noticed an unusual ring, most likely custom made. *A coat of arms?* She looked closer as the hand seemed to magnify just enough for her to see what the vision intended—a family crest.

Message received.

It was sometime during the night, summer flipped to fall. Colbie noticed the morning air no longer felt sultry as she stepped onto the tiny balcony off of her room, a cup of hot tea in hand.

It was early—after her visions the previous night, she barely slept, eager to tell Ryan about the new lead in their investigation. Well, it wasn't a lead, really—but, it was a new avenue to explore. Exactly what the crest on the ring meant, she had no idea—but, she did know it probably wouldn't be too difficult to trace.

She pulled her cell from her bathrobe pocket, then tapped Ryan's number with her thumb. Although he didn't know it yet, researching Georgia family crests was first on his list of things to do.

"Good God! Do you know what time it is?" Ryan's voice was gravelly and scratchy with sleep.

"I do. It's exactly five-thirty-three—why aren't you up?"

A momentary silence, then a gut laugh. "Ouch! Okay—you're right! Damn it! I should be up, showered, and dressed by now! You know you're making me look bad, don't you?"

"My intention, of course . . ."

She waited a few seconds until he was ready to talk. "Change in plans for this morning . . ."

"You mean, I'm off Buford Collins?"

"Yep—we need to research Georgia family crests."

"What? Why?"

A brief pause. "Well, after you left last night . . ."

"You mean after you kicked me out . . ."

Colbie let that ride, refusing to give him the satisfaction. "Like I was saying, we need to research them because I had a vision—I saw a crest on a ring on a woman's index finger."

"How do you know it was a woman?"

"Well, the beautifully manicured gel fingernails were my first clue . . ."

"Gel . . ."

"Never mind—that's not important. What *is* important is the crest."

Ryan sat up, propping up three pillows against the headboard. "What did it look like?"

"It was like two, old-fashioned, silver cups welded together in the center, the handles to the sides."

Ryan didn't say anything, trying to visualize her description. "Like medieval cups?"

"Not cups, really—more like silver challises . . ."

"You mean like from Ireland or England—somewhere over there?"

"Precisely!"

"Okay—what does the crest have to do with anything? And, what do you think it has to do with the Clyburns, Mariska, in particular?"

"I'm not sure, but that's what we have to find out . . ."

CHAPTER

14

assius Sprague sat across from Monroe Clyburn, a fine, Cuban cigar held firmly in his fingers— since Monroe indulged, he figured he could, too. "How's Agatha," he asked, not really caring, yet knowing he should extend the courtesy. The sad truth was there wasn't much Sprague cared about other than his business, and that translated into money.

Both comfortable in sitting-room chairs, Clyburn stared at him for a moment trying to figure out why a man who hated him popped in, unannounced. At the office, it would have been strange enough—but, at his home?

"She's . . . fine, I suppose. Although, I don't know how fine one can be after losing a child . . ."

Sprague nodded. "I can't imagine . . ."

Clyburn waited for a few moments, finally deciding enough was enough. "So, Cassius—to what do I owe the pleasure?"

"I apologize for dropping by without notice—please apologize to Agatha for me. But, I had to know . . ."

"Know what?"

A brief silence. "Did you get a call?"

Monroe noticed his guest was clearly uneasy. "A call? From whom?"

"That's just it—I don't know . . ."

"What did the caller say?"

Cassius ashed his cigar, noting his vice wasn't well accepted by most people, except Monroe. "A filthy habit, my wife tells me—daily. " He paused. "It was a warning . . ."

"A warning? About what?"

"That's just it—I'm not really sure. The call lasted about ten seconds, and that was it. Just a warning that things were about to change . . ."

Both men sat quietly, thinking about who would be so foolish to cross either of them.

"A threat," Monroe asked, mentally ticking off those whom he considered stupid enough to do such a thing.

"Not in so many words—but, the implication was clear."

"Collins?"

"Buford Collins?" Sprague looked at his colleague, slightly astonished. "Why him?"

"Well, there was the buyout . . ." Sprague decided it wasn't prudent to discuss his conversation with Collins at the golf club months prior.

"The buyout? That was years ago! Besides, there isn't a soul alive who knows . . ."

"Still—he always struck me as . . ." Monroe paused, trying to think of the right word. "Pedestrian . . ."

"I can't argue that—and, he's no different now than he was back in the day . . ."

Clyburn fell quiet, again thinking. "I still don't get what this has to do with me . . ."

Sprague nodded. "It may not—I was just curious, that's all . . ."

Neither wanted to acknowledge it would have been easier and more comfortable if Sprague would simply have called rather than making the trip to the elite suburbs. Monroe Clyburn knew him to be direct, and to the point in personal as well as business situations—so, a drop in?

Completely out of character.

A mediocre breakfast later, Colbie and Ryan divvied up what they needed to accomplish, going their separate ways after agreeing to touch base in early afternoon. Tasked with researching the family crest, he headed to the library while Kevin and Colbie headed to Mariska's university alma mater.

"What do you hope to find out when we get there?" Kevin glanced in the rearview mirror, then at her.

Colbie didn't look up from her notes. "Honestly, I'm not sure. There's a huge disconnect in Mariska Clyburn's murder and, so far, we have ideas, but no suspects. That has to change!"

Kevin nodded. "What ideas?"

Colbie grinned, looking at him. "I was afraid you were going to ask me that . . ."

"Ah—no ideas?"

"Not really . . ."

"Well, maybe Mariska's college days will reveal something—but, it's been several years since she graduated, so it might be tough finding anyone who knew her . . ."

"I know—it makes me wonder, though . . ."

"Wonder what?"

"Well—why didn't she go to the same college as her parents? These days, admission can be decided strictly based on legacy . . ."

"From what I knew about Mariska, a smaller college was much more her style—her parents, however, a totally different story. I heard Agatha brag more than once how she was revered in her sorority, the envy of her sisters . . ."

Colbie glanced at him, then stared out the window. "Do you know where Agatha went to school?"

"Yep—in fact, it's not far from here. Maybe two hours, tops . . ."

She didn't say anything for a few moments, trying to resolve a gut feeling. "Let's head there . . ."

Something was off—something didn't feel right as Ryan stood at a crossroad, looking up the street for any indication he was in the right area. Spanish moss hung from trees, filtering autumn light through twisted branches, some forming a canopy over the narrow, two-lane road. *This can't be right*, he thought as he checked his phone for the right address for a woman who was supposed to know everything about old Savannah. Miss Carlisle—as she was known by locals—was a walking encyclopedia when it came to her town's history, and there wasn't a thing she didn't know.

That was according to the librarian.

It was when he glanced up trying to get his bearings, he noticed a familiar figure walking into the shade of moss-laden trees fifty yards up the road. *What the hell?* He squinted, trying to focus on the squatty, dumpy little man disappearing through a spired gate.

What the hell is Buford Collins doing here?

"Dean Beddington? I'm Colbie Colleen—thanks for seeing me on such short notice!" Colbie extended her hand, appreciating his firm grip.

"Not at all—but, I don't have much time. As you can see, we're back in the swing . . ."

"I noticed! It's been a long time since I was on a college campus . . ." She paused. "But, it's nice to know things haven't changed!"

Ernest Beddington laughed, offering her a chair in front of his desk. His office was the epitome of a college professor's—books lined mahogany shelves, and files were stacked on his desk, all demanding attention. "Indeed— little has changed here for the last hundred years. Except technology, of course!"

Colbie agreed, taking in everything she could see. "I'll try not to take up too much of your time," she began, looking directly at him. "I'm a private investigator, and I'm working on a case out of Savannah . . ."

Beddington's eyebrows arched. "An investigator? Good heavens! What help can I possibly be?"

"Well, I'm not sure—I'll be the first to admit I'm on a fishing expedition. So . . . knowing that, how long have you been the dean here?"

"Seven years—why?"

Colbie paused, thinking. "Do you have a good handle on university history?"

"I'm not sure what you mean . . ."

"I'm sorry—I'm not being very clear. Since, in the great scheme of things, you haven't been in your position long, what do you know about the university's past?"

Dean Beddington's right eye twitched slightly with mounting impatience. "If there's something in particular you want to know, Miss Colleen, just say it . . ."

Colbie smiled. "You're right—what do you know about a murder here about forty years ago?"

"Murder? Here?"

"Oh, yes—like I said, about forty years ago. Her name was Gracie Brightwood . . ." Colbie, of course, had no intention of telling him Gracie's death was never attributed to murder—she dropped the 'm' word only to get his serious attention.

"I'm afraid I can't be of any help—I don't know of any murder . . ."

"Does the name Agatha Culpepper sound familiar?"

Beddington thought for a moment. "Culpepper? No—I can't say it does . . ."

"What about Monroe Clyburn?"

Beddington was still for a moment, unsure of his response. One not to believe in coincidence, it became instantly clear the phone call he received had something to do with the lovely Colbie Colleen's sitting across from him. "Well . . ."

Colbie noticed his hesitation. "Do you know Monroe Clyburn?"

He glanced at her, then focused on the calendar on his desk, still deciding if he should mention the call. "Not really—I've heard of him, however."

"Heard of him, how?"

The stately dean shifted in his chair, eyes cast down as if in thought. "I received a call . . ."

Colbie didn't allow a second to pass. "From whom?"

"That's just it—I don't know . . ." He looked up, fully aware Colbie was relentlessly focused on everything coming out of his mouth.

"What did the caller say?"

Beddington hesitated. When he told his wife about the call, he didn't quite tell her everything. "It was weird—almost like a clue . . ."

Colbie kept her eyes on his. "Do you remember what it was?"

"Oh, yes—I remember it well. The voice said . . ."

"Male or female?"

"Disguised."

Colbie nodded. "Sorry—please continue . . ."

The dean looked at her, then recited, verbatim, the caller's words.

Of decades past, you do not know.
Of people present, a formidable foe.
Beware of changes yet to be,
History talks, and you will see.

Colbie stared, processing what she just heard. "Seriously? It sounds like a poem—or, a clue . . ."

"Indeed—that's how I memorized it quickly. Who knew an emphasis in poetry while completing my masters would come in handy . . ."

"You have to admit, it's a little creepy . . ."

"More than a 'little' creepy, Ms. Colleen . . ."

"Did the caller say anything else?"

Again, Beddinton's eyes met hers. "Monroe Clyburn."

"What about him?"

"That was it—just his name."

Both sat silently, Colbie trying to fit pieces together, the dean wishing she would leave. "Do you know what it means," he finally asked.

She shook her head. "No, but it has to mean something!"

For the next ten minutes, Colbie wrote down the poem, asking questions, hoping to augment what she just learned. But, it wasn't meant to be—Dean Beddington ended their conversation, speaking of an upcoming appointment, gently guiding her toward his office door. There was no mistaking he preferred she investigate somewhere else—no offer of helping in any way he could, or an obligatory invitation to contact him whenever.

No, he never wanted to see Colbie Colleen again.

CHAPTER

15

While Colbie was attempting to unravel the poetic mystery, Ryan—as inconspicuously as possible—strolled down the road as if he were a tourist. It was a tactic that didn't make much sense, but, if asked, he could, at least, admit he was lost. One might believe it, too, for there was nothing of interest anywhere in sight.

As he rounded the gentle, left-leaning curve of the two-lane road, he noticed a BMW sports car parked on one side, a small house with a spired fence and gate on the other. It creeped him out, and he couldn't help thinking of the medieval fence in the movie, *The Omen*. Even at first glance, he knew there was nothing good in that small home, and he didn't want to find out if he were right.

A quick scan memorized the BMW's license plate, and he was about to head back to his car when a woman called to him from the front porch. "May I be of assistance? You appear lost . . ."

Ryan turned to see a striking woman with raven hair standing on the front porch of the small cottage—her right hand poised on a small column at the top of wooden steps, a large ring on her index finger glinting in the sunlight.

"Well, I sure got turned around somewhere!"

"Do you have a car?"

"I do . . ." He pointed down the road, then returned his attention to her. "You don't happen to know a . . . Miss Carlisle, do you?"

"Anna Lee? Why, of course! Everybody knows her . . ." For the first time, she eyed him with suspicion. "She doesn't live anywhere around here . . ."

Ryan shot her his most engaging smile. "I figured that out!" He waited, hoping she would invite him in for an iced tea—or, something. "Do you know where she lives?"

The woman looked him up and down. "What's your business with Miss Carlisle?"

"I'm researching my family's crest—you know, a coat of arms—and, the librarian told me Miss Carlisle is the person who knows everything about Savannah history . . ."

Nice save.

Suddenly, the woman laughed, gesturing for him to join her. "I can draw you a map . . ."

Ryan didn't waste any time bolting through the gate and up the rickety steps, extending his hand. If everything went his way, he'd get a glimpse at the ring, and find out who owned the BMW.

She accepted his hand, then suddenly pulled back, both unaware of eyes peering at them from behind the living room curtains. "Who are you," she asked, her eyes growing colder by the second.

"Geez—I'm sorry! I should have introduced myself—my name is Ryan—Ryan Fitzpatrick." For some reason, his gut was telling him it wasn't the time for a fictitious character. There was something about the woman making him uneasy, and he had no doubt as they stood together on the small veranda, she was a formidable force. "Look, I'm sorry—I'm sure I'll find it, eventually! Thanks for the offer, though . . ."

With that, he was down the steps and through the gate, refusing to look back.

Ernest Beddington waited until he was certain Colbie was out of the building before instructing his secretary he wasn't taking calls for the next hour. The investigator's visit was unnerving, and it wasn't fitting for anyone to see him other than as professorial at all times. He was, in fact, the epitome of a university dean—staid in all he said and did, rarely allowing anyone see another side of him.

The truth was things were getting out of hand.

"Who was that?"

"He said his name is Ryan Fitzpatrick . . ."

Buford Collins eyed the woman. "Do you know him?"

She shook her head. "No—at least, not in the way you mean." She glanced at the front porch, then at Collins. "The one I told you about? She's with him . . ."

Buford barely breathed.

"If your plans aren't finalized, I suggest you do so—you have little time."

Grabbing his driving gloves, Collins stormed toward the door, clutching its handle for a moment. Then, he turned toward the woman who knew him better than anyone. "How long?"

"Soon. Very soon . . ."

Ryan filled Colbie in that evening and, when she heard of the woman with the jet-black hair, she knew instantly the connection wasn't good. "You did the right thing by getting the hell out of there," she commented. "She's in this . . ."

"I gotta tell ya—I'm not certain I know what 'this' is, anymore. I'm beginning to feel as if I need to create a spreadsheet just to keep track . . ."

Colbie grinned. "That might not be a bad idea!"

"So—what about you? Did you learn anything?"

"Oh, yes! Prop your feet up because you're going to love this!"

For the next hour Colbie recounted her visit with Dean Beddington, recalling the conversation word-for-word. When finished, she poured both of them a glass of wine. "For the first time in months," she commented, "I feel as if we made progress—and, for the first time, I think we're heading in the right direction."

Ryan was quiet, then asked the obvious. "Which direction?"

"Until telling me about your encounter with the woman with black hair, I wasn't sure. Now, I am . . ."

"And?"

"Buford Collins—he's the main player."

"But, why? I'm still not getting the connection . . ."

"I didn't mention it before, but, when I was opening my intuition last night? I saw the woman you met today—she's a powerful psychic, not to be underestimated . . ."

"And, don't forget about the ring—even though I didn't get a good look at it, I'm sure it's the one you saw . . ."

"As am I . . ."

Throughout the last several years, Ryan knew Colbie's visions were accurate, as well as her interpretations. "That's not good news . . ." He paused, rearranging puzzle pieces in his brain. "So—I'll bet when I ask my guy at the department to run the plate, we'll know for sure if the BMW is the same one we saw at the funeral—and, if it belongs to Collins. And, we'll know for sure, he's meeting with her because I saw him as he walked toward the gate. But, he was fairly far away, so I couldn't swear to it—but, the question is why?"

"Who knows? But, my gut tells me she's driving the bus on something, and that something involves Collins, Clyburn, and Ernest Beddington—a few more might surface, as well. All we have to do is connect the dots . . ."

"What about Beulah Brightwood? What does she have to do with it?"

Colbie thought for a moment. "Good question—I'm not ruling her out simply because she knows Collins. We know that for sure . . . but, is she involved?"

"Well, I hope we figure it out soon. I'm tired of running in circles . . ."

"We will. I can tell you one thing, though . . ."

"What's that?"

"It's all about revenge . . ."

CHAPTER

16

onroe Clyburn sat in his favorite chair in the study, thinking. He didn't like Sprague's stopping by unannounced the previous evening—but, when he listened to the reason for the surprise visit, he wasn't so sure he wouldn't have done the same were the tables reversed. *Sprague's a lot of things,* he thought, *but he's not a coward. Telling me about the call? Nothing more than his forging an alliance, if needed . . .*

Chilling rain splatted against the window, no end in sight and, in such weather, Agatha always suffered migraines—that day was no different. Bidding her husband an early goodnight, she retired to sleep off the rigors of her day, praying the pain would be gone when she awakened.

So, there he sat, two drinks in, thinking about his wife—the woman he loved more than anything, or anyone. Since Mariska's death, her ability to cope with daily life was spiraling downward—but, then again, he noticed little effort on her part.

And, that was a problem.

When they met, decades ago, Agatha Culpepper was a young, confident woman who knew what she wanted, and how to get it. It was an attitude serving her well throughout life, but, since Mariska's passing? Society engagements were in the toilet and, worse, she didn't care. There was little impetus to get her out of the house and, after a couple of months of playing the shrinking violet, her dyed-in-the-wool friends started looking elsewhere for scintillating conversation. Although Monroe never considered his wife's newfound fragility an issue, the possibility of her needing professional help was definitely on his radar.

Those thoughts, however, were for a different time.

More pressing was Sprague's mysterious phone call—it didn't make sense, but, as long as his name wasn't mentioned, he supposed it didn't matter. There was nothing in his past that could come back to bite him in the ass, so he really could care less.

Still . . .

"We're out of time—everything goes into motion immediately . . ."

"Why? What happened?"

"Someone's snooping around—and, according to Morgan, we don't have much time . . ."

Beulah's eyes narrowed as she noticed a mix of fear and resolve deep in her step-brother's eyes. "Who?" Instantly, her mind tracked back to the woman and young man who turned on the wrong road and sat in her parlor, drinking her tea.

"He said his name was Ryan Fitzpatrick . . ."

"Fitzpatrick . . ." She let the name rest on her tongue as she recalled her two visitors. "That wasn't the name . . ."

"Whose name?"

Exasperated, Beulah hoisted herself out of one of the overstuffed chairs, then headed for the kitchen. "You remember those two people who said they were looking for Magnolia Road—I told you about that . . ."

"Yeah—what about it? What does that . . ." Then, the light bulb. "You mean, you think they're the same people Morgan warned me about?" He stared at her, not liking the look in her eyes.

After rifling through the refrigerator for something tasty and loaded with calories, she emerged with ice cream and chocolate sauce. "Want some?"

"No—I'm good . . ."

Between the time Buford walked in the door and Beulah's offering him a snack, perspiration began to bead on his forehead. He didn't like being rushed, preferring to carry out personal plans or business dealings knowing the intended outcome. He thought he had at least a month to get his ducks in a row before following through on what he determined would be the most glorious moment of his life. His dream. His calling.

Everything—until then—was progressing as planned, but, now? Things were going to shit, and there wasn't a damned thing he could do about it.

Beulah sat on the couch so she could face him, diving into two scoops and a swimming pool of hot fudge sauce. "Have you waited long enough?"

Collins was silent for a moment, then answered, his voice low in case anyone happened to be lurking in the dying bushes outside the living room window. "That's just it—I'm not sure. Headlines died down, but, you never know . . ."

His step-sister dabbed at a trickle of errant chocolate sauce on the corner of her lip. "What does Morgan say?"

"She says I'm still in danger . . ."

"Only you?"

"I didn't ask about anyone else."

She shot him a look, wondering if it were too late to back out. "That was big of you . . ."

Buford remained silent, one thing on his mind.

It was time.

Ernest Beddington adored the campus library, the scent of aging leather and paper adding to its overall ambiance of comfort and feeling like home. It was where he spent time when troubled—much like a church to many—and, he couldn't shake the feeling something was about to break loose. Normally, he would have dismissed such a thought, but, after the ominous call and Colbie Colleen's spontaneous visit?

Something was going to hit the fan.

As he headed for the stacks containing written history of the school, thoughts turned to Monroe Clyburn. Although it was in his best interest to maintain they never met, it was a fact far from the truth, their acquaintanceship going back to the year he accepted the appointment as Dean. It was then they entered into a dark agreement—one guaranteed to pay well simply for maintaining the status quo.

Monroe's was a generous offer, one which Beddington couldn't resist. After all, maintaining the lifestyle of such an esteemed position cost money—far more than he could earn on a yearly salary. When Monroe placed terms of their agreement in front of him in the form of cold cash?

A clandestine partnership was born.

His footsteps echoed on the marble floor, no sound of students to absorb his preferred secrecy. It was ironic he never considered researching why Monroe wanted all talk of his attending the university hushed before it got started. If anyone got the silly idea of a 'Successful Alumni Day,' his name would never be put in the pot for consideration.

Of course, digital media wasn't in anyone's thoughts during the time of hippies and personal liberation, so scrolling through microfiche articles regarding the university's and town's history proved a laborious process, and it wasn't until his watch clicked just past ten, he found it. The article.

The reason Monroe Clyburn didn't want anyone, anywhere, breathing a word . . .

CHAPTER

17

That evening, rain morphed into a freezing drizzle, topping it with a skiff of snow—a rarity in the Deep South. Agatha Clyburn sat up in bed, mascara tears streaking her face as she shrieked to the apparition standing at the base of her bed. "I didn't mean to! I swear! I didn't mean to!" Her screams turned to whimpers as she realized her protestations didn't mean crap—they didn't change a thing.

A dark mist shadowing the bedroom door joined the figure standing in front of Agatha, her eyes wide with astonished fear. Both were wet, straggling wisps of hair plastered to their faces, eyes vacant and accusing, and it was her final shriek prompting Monroe off of his feet, and up the stairs. Fearing the worst, he burst through the door to see his wife crumpled on the bed, sobbing. "Do you see them," she asked through choking tears.

Quickly, he scanned the room as he helped her swing her legs to the side of the bed, offering her a glass of water. "See who?"

"Them! Mariska! Mariska and . . ."

It was then she disintegrated, sorrow consuming her thoughts. Words.

Soul.

The freak snow storm—if it could be considered as such—halted ground transport, jamming highways and side streets, making for the perfect evening to stay in with a cup of hot chocolate and a movie. The movie was the easy part—hot chocolate? Not so much.

"I finally got this powdered stuff," Ryan commented as he pulled groceries for an evening snack from a paper bag. "I can't believe it's so stinkin' hard to find!"

Colbie grinned. "Gee, I don't know—do you think the fact this is Savannah might have something to do with it?"

"Hot chocolate should be available everywhere, any time of the year," he laughed as he grabbed two cups from the cabinet beside the small fridge. "And, I don't mind telling you, I'm ready to stop living out of a hotel! What I'd give for my tiny kitchen in my tiny apartment . . ."

"I know—if I were to be completely honest, I miss Seattle—the smell of the Sound . . ."

Ryan stopped opening the hot chocolate can, looking at her. "What are you going to do?"

"You mean when our case is over?"

"Yeah—are you going back to Seattle?"

Colbie shrugged. "I guess—although there's nothing there for me . . ."

"You mean, Brian . . ."

For the first time mentioning his name, her eyes didn't brim with tears. "Well, yeah—Tammy's not there, either, so I'm not sure what I'm going to do . . ."

Without looking at her, Ryan heard the indecision in her voice, unsure of how to comfort her. "Well—you don't have to decide now. That's the good news!"

"Is there bad news?"

He checked the counter, then the paper bag. "I forgot the whipped cream—but, I remembered the popcorn!"

Five minutes later, both were parked on the couch, ready to relax. "While you were gone," Colbie mentioned, "I got a really weird feeling about Agatha Clyburn . . ."

"What kind of feeling?"

"Not good, I can tell you that—but, what I saw was weird. It was a spinning pinwheel with Mariska's face smack in the middle of it . . ."

Ryan stopped fishing in the popcorn bag, looking at her. "That's creepy—you mean, like one of those pinwheels you'd get at a fair, or something?"

"The same . . ."

"I don't get it—what's the connection?"

"I have no idea—but, that does bring me to something else. After meeting with Ernest Beddington, I'm convinced he didn't tell me everything . . ."

"Like what?"

"Well, he didn't tell me much except about the caller who warned him things are going to change . . ."

"So?"

"So . . . why would anyone call the dean of a university with such a warning? Unless . . ."

Ryan picked up the thread. "Unless, he either knows something, or is involved in something . . ."

"Exactly. No one is going to do such a thing unless there's involvement in some way . . ."

"I get it—but, it's supposition, and finding out if you're right isn't going to be easy."

Colbie thought for a minute. "I know . . ."

She opened one eye, glaring at her cell vibrating on the nightstand. Three buzzes later, she answered. "Ryan? This better be good . . ."

"It's not Ryan—it's Kevin. Did you hear?"

Colbie sat up, her mind at full attention. "No—hear what?"

"Are you sitting down?"

"Of course, I'm sitting down! I was asleep!"

"Right. Sorry . . ."

Colbie flicked on the light. "Okay—what's so important you had to call me at . . . six o'clock?"

"Monroe . . ."

"What about him?"

"He was found floating in the River Styx!" Colbie had been in Savannah long enough to know that particular river flowed into the swamp—a place where nothing good happened.

"What? How do you know?"

"It was on the morning news—there's no mistake, Colbie. It's him . . ."

"Holy shit! What else? Do they know anything?"

"Not much—some moron who was running on icy roads found him about two o'clock this morning."

"Two o'clock? In crappy weather? That doesn't sound right . . ."

"That's what I thought . . ."

Both were quiet for a moment until Colbie rang off, calling Ryan the second she disconnected. She filled him in on what she knew, both agreeing to meet in the hotel restaurant at eight-o'clock.

"This changes everything, you know," he commented before hanging up.

"In a way—but, if the authorities conclude Clyburn was murdered, the killer just tipped his hand . . ."

"Meaning?"

"I'll tell you at breakfast . . ."

Ernest Bedding arrived at the breakfast table looking restrained as ever, dutifully placing a quick peck on his wife's cheek as he flicked the television on with the remote. "I can't remember seeing so much snow in Georgia," he commented as his wife slapped two waffles topped with blueberries on a plate, then set it at his usual place at the table. "I know! Two inches? I heard schools are closed . . ."

"Beats the hell out of St. Louis, doesn't it?" He laughed, recalling miserable winters when snow stayed on the ground for months, eventually morphing into a lovely shade of dirt brown mixed with bits of windshield-shattering gravel.

"I don't know how we stood it for so long!" She joined him at the table, her own plate graced with only one waffle, and a few, anemic-looking blueberries, the last from the package. "Why were you so late last night?" She glanced at him as she poured the syrup.

"Late? Really?"

"I heard you come in—it was well past midnight."

Beddington took a bite. "Well, you know me—I was at the library until late, researching for my novel."

Mary Ellen paused, mid-bite. "You've been working on that thing for years—will it ever be done?"

"Soon—very soon."

"That's what you always say . . ."

"I know—but, last night, I think I had a breakthrough. It was the last bit of research before I write the ending . . ."

With that, he ratcheted up the television's volume, eyes glued to a body being hauled from the River Styx. "The body of Monroe Clyburn was discovered a little after two this morning by a jogger . . ."

Mary Ellen stared at the television, then at her husband. "Monroe Clyburn? We were just talking about him not too long ago!"

"Indeed, we were . . ."

The nasally voice of the news reporter grated on his nerves, especially so early in the morning—still, he increased the volume. "With no identification, it was only by luck the jogger recognized the body as Clyburn's . . ."

Ernest and Mary Ellen watched as recorded footage showed emergency personnel guiding a gurney loaded with a body bag toward an ambulance. "An ambulance? Was he alive when they showed up?" She turned to her husband, perplexed.

"Who knows? Probably precaution . . ."

"Well, it's pretty weird if you ask me. I can't imagine Monroe Clyburn was out at that time of night during a freak snowstorm because he felt like getting some fresh air." She paused as an errant blueberry rolled across her plate, finally stopping at the edge of a pool of syrup. "Something stinks." Another pause. "Something really stinks . . ."

Her husband was quiet as the on-location news segment ended, then promised a return to a less gruesome topic— Georgia weather. Without comment, he rose, pushing his chair into the table as his mother taught him so many years prior. "I have to go . . ."

"What? It's early!"

"I know, but we have campus guests today, and I need to get my work done before they arrive . . ."

"Don't forget to take your coat—I feel a chill!"

"See you at dinner," he promised, kissing the top of her head. "Be good!"

She laughed, loving the intimacy of their private lives

for just a moment. It was a directive he'd been giving her since they married, never missing a day. Little did she know—or, suspect—the chill she spoke of had nothing to do with Georgia's fickle weather . . .

It was the frigid chill of deception.

A cup of tea in front of her, Colbie waited for Ryan, thinking about the news of Clyburn's death. It didn't take a genius to figure out foul play was to blame, but she couldn't be sure until she knew more. Thinking about the possibilities, she didn't notice him until he pulled out a chair at their table.

"Hey, you! No booth?"

She grinned, scanning the restaurant. "Look at this place! It's packed! Due to the weather, I'm guessing . . ."

He took off his jacket, hanging it on the back of his chair. "No doubt—although, even though the sun's barely up, it's already starting to warm . . ."

Moments later, he sat across from her, a cup of coffee heating his hands. "So—I watched the news. What do you think?"

Colbie shook her head. "Damned if I know . . . but, I don't think there's any doubt Monroe Clyburn was murdered."

"According to the news, they don't know anything . . ."

"True, but think about it—with everything we uncovered over the last days and weeks, I know for a fact he wouldn't be out in such weather if he didn't have to . . ." She paused. "And, with what Ernest Beddington told us? I'm betting something's coming to a head . . ."

Ryan leveled a serious look. "Maybe. You know it won't take the cops long to find out you were investigating his daughter's disappearance . . ."

"And, they'll ask me about her murder . . ."

"True—but, you don't know anything about that."

"Still, detectives worth their salt are going to research me, and they'll find out what I do for a living. They're going to want to know everything . . ."

"So . . . do you think Monroe's murder—if that's what it turns out to be—is related to Mariska's?"

"Her murder?" Colbie paused. "Well, yes—but, there's something telling me the connection is convoluted. Like there isn't a clear path between the two . . ."

"There hasn't been a clear path to anything in this investigation, if you ask me!"

"You're right about that . . ."

After a moment's silence, Ryan signaled the server for a refill, then refocused on Colbie. "You said Monroe's murderer tipped his hand—how?"

"It's too close on the heels of the phone call to Ernest Beddington . . ."

Ryan nodded, thinking for a few seconds before continuing Colbie's thought. "And, you said you think Beddington knows more than he's letting on . . ."

"I still do—but, does that mean he knows anything about Clyburn's murder?" She didn't wait for an answer. "Not necessarily . . ."

"I must be dense, but I don't see the connection. But, there must be one—otherwise, why would anyone make a disguised phone call mentioning Clyburn's name?"

"That's what I keep asking—and, the answer is always the same. As sure as I'm sitting here, Ernest Beddington knows something, and he just rose to the top of my list."

"For what"

"For . . . well, I'm not sure yet. But, I'll get to the bottom of it, I promise you that . . ."

Within two hours of first broadcast news, Agatha Clyburn was hospitalized. She, too, heard of her husband's demise on the morning reports, not afforded the courtesy of a personal visit by Savannah's finest. No—she learned of it while in her designer bathrobe and slippers, sipping a cup of fine, Kona coffee strong enough to strip the hair from any man's chest.

Her boys were at her side within the half hour, both devastated not only by their father's passing, but also by their mother's mental fracturing. When they found her, she lay crumpled on the floor, her face ashen, eyes hollowing as they watched her slip further into some sort of deep psychosis. By the time they whisked her from camera lens's prying eyes, she didn't recognize Marcus or Melbourne, only calling her husband's name.

And, Mariska's.

CHAPTER

18

As Colbie surmised, detectives were on her hotel doorstep within the week, asking about everything regarding her relationship with Monroe Clyburn. Had she been an inexperienced private investigator, she may have felt intimidated by their direct questioning. But, after the first few questions, she realized they were in the same boat as Ryan and she—although, they knew less simply because they were in the neophyte stages of their investigation. Immediately, she pegged both of them to be intelligent, representing the best of Savannah's police department.

By the time they wrapped up, detectives knew not only salient points of Colbie's investigation into Mariska's disappearance, but her suspicions of Ernest Beddington, as well. "I haven't put everything together, but my gut tells me he knows something . . ."

The detective with shaved, blond hair glanced at his partner, then focused again on Colbie. "You think Ernest Beddington murdered Monroe Clyburn?"

She shook her head. "I didn't say that—I only meant I think he knows more than he's saying. Now, if that includes anything about a murder, I don't know . . ."

"How many times?"

"I'm not sure I follow . . ."

"How many times did you meet with Beddington?"

"Just once."

"Only once, and you think he has information?" The detective, appearing in his mid-forties, snickered. As far as he was concerned, he didn't believe in intuitive crap—it either was or wasn't, and gut feelings didn't amount to much.

Colbie's eyes darkened. "I take it you don't have much respect—or, knowledge—about what I do, Detective . . ."

"Dellinger. Damion Dellinger—I mentioned it when we arrived."

"So you did . . ."

Ryan sat silently, knowing Colbie's ability to verbally annihilate anyone when provoked—glancing at her, it was quickly becoming one of those times. "What do you know about Brightwood Pharmaceuticals," he asked, deflecting attention away from her.

Detective Dellinger's eyes flickered with interest. "Not much—it's nothing when compared to Clyburn's outfit. Why?"

"What about Buford Collins?"

Detective Dellinger thought for a moment, then glanced at his partner. "Collins? Not a whole lot . . ." He paused, then focused on Colbie. "Tell me what you know . . ."

Another hour passed as Colbie and Ryan recounted Colbie's and Kevin's chance meeting with Beulah Brightwood and Ryan's run in with the psychic, as well as his knowing—suspecting—Buford Collins was at her place for whatever reason.

"Was the woman's name Morgan," Detective Dellinger asked.

Ryan shrugged. "I don't know, but as soon as she shook my hand, I got the creeps—that's all I can tell you. She gave me a look that would shrivel anyone, and I got the hell out of there . . ."

"Who's Morgan?" Colbie glanced at Ryan, then at the detective. "Obviously, you have an idea of who Ryan saw that day . . ."

Dellinger nodded. "Morgan Stratford—she's been around these parts for as long as I can remember, and I've been here twenty-five years."

"What about her?"

"Well, nothing, really—she's the psychic for Savannah's elite, and she plays the part twenty-four hours a day . . ."

"Meaning?"

"Oh, you know—large, hoop earrings, black, flowing-type skirts . . ."

"She looks like a damned witch!" Dellinger's partner shuddered as he thought of her. "I don't care what you say—there's something wrong with someone like that . . ."

Colbie glanced at Ryan. "Do you remember when I told you I felt as if someone were watching Kevin and me when we pulled out of Beulah's lane the first time we were there? When we trailed Collins? Maybe it was her . . ."

"How could I forget?"

She returned her attention to both detectives, leveling a look at each. "It makes no difference to me whether you believe in what I do, or not—what does make a difference, however, is my doing the job I came to do . . ."

"And, what is that, again?"

"Mariska Clyburn's murder. And, I know, without question, our top players are Ernest Beddington, Beulah Brightwood, and Buford Collins." She paused, thinking. "Something ties them together . . ."

"And, you think that's Monroe Clyburn?"

Colbie nodded. "That's my gut. But, I'm not one hundred percent certain—and, I have to be before making such an assertion . . ."

Detective Dellinger decided it wasn't the time to bring up his personal beliefs. "What do you suggest?"

"We work together—but, not really . . ."

"Not really?"

Colbie squared her body in her chair as if poised to do battle. "You'll be wise not to forget about Morgan—she's a considerable force."

Ryan sat up and leaned forward, resting his forearms on his knees. "But what does she have to do with everything? Maybe she's just someone Collins knows—maybe she doesn't have anything to do with this . . ."

Colbie didn't take her eyes from him. "She's the one driving the bus . . ."

It didn't take long for the press to get wind of Agatha's admittance to the psych ward in the only hospital Savanna's social set deemed suitable. As soon as Monroe's murder hit the airwaves? Reporters and photographers swarmed the Clyburn estate's wrought iron gates, but, what they hoped to see, one couldn't be sure—everyone living there, with the exception of Agatha, was dead.

It was a stark realization and, once made, tongues wagged. As you can well imagine, admittance to a mental facility was something unspeakable—families in the five million and up crowd refused to acknowledge she was one of them and, other than Marcus and Melbourne being at her side, no one seemed to care. Officially?

She was off their list.

The sad thing was—once Agatha realized where she was and the reason why—she knew her days as one of Savannah's preferred socialites were history. The life as she knew it was over, never to be retrieved and, most likely, it was one of the reasons for her fracturing.

It was two weeks before Detective Dellinger and his partner could speak to her, doctors purposely keeping her cloistered knowing her fragile condition. Receiving the hospital's best care, there were private meetings with remaining family members to discuss the next step—and, that was something Dellinger suspected, prompting the unannounced visit to the quiet east wing. "I don't give a crap what they say—I'm talking to her. If they don't like it, they can kiss my ass . . ."

Knowing fully aware his partner was in one of his moods, Detective Jonathan Baker barely nodded. They'd been stymied by everything Monroe, and those who were the Clyburn's friends weren't inclined to divulge what they knew—about anything. Dellinger considered it obstruction while the upper crust considered it good taste—that, and not wanting to be involved.

Anna Lee Carlisle sat, placing her cup and saucer on the hand carved coffee table in front of her. Ryan wasn't sure what he expected, but, at first glance, when she opened the door, she dripped southern class. Premature white hair pulled softly back in a perfect bun, she exuded the charm for which Savannah was so well known, her lanky stature framed beautifully by a perfectly tailored suit. Age? Maybe sixty-five—seventy, tops.

"Now, Mr. Fitzpatrick—what can I do for you?"

Ryan smiled. "Well, I'm not sure—but, I'm hoping you can fill me in on Savannah history . . ."

Anna Lee eyed him carefully. "What kind of history?"

He paused, considering the consequences if he didn't level with her. "My partner and I are investigating a murder— I'm sure you've heard about it . . ."

No reaction. "Why don't you enlighten me?"

"Several months ago, my partner was hired to investigate what happened to Mariska Clyburn . . ."

"Oh, yes—that was so sad. And, her father, too!"

Ryan watched her expression soften at the reference to Monroe Clyburn. "Did you know him?"

"Monroe?" She didn't wait for Ryan to confirm. "My land, yes! He and I went to school together, although I was several grades ahead of him."

"Did you know him well?"

"Well enough— as children, he and my youngest brother were inseparable."

Anna Lee sat back in her chair, quietly thinking for a moment or two. "What is it you need to know, Mr. Fitzpatrick?"

"It's my understanding you know everything about Savannah history, so I need you to take me back in time . . ."

"How far?"

"To the time you knew Monroe . . ."

She was quiet for a moment. "I don't know if I can help, but he had quite the reputation with the ladies, I can tell you that!"

Ryan smiled, relaxing into his chair. Anna Lee Carlisle was, apparently, open to giving him the information he needed, and he planned to take advantage of every second with her. "Really? I never had the pleasure of meeting him, but he certainly must have caught Agatha's eye!"

"Oh, yes—and, once Monroe set his sights on her, there was no going back."

"Do you know Agatha?"

"Not well—there was never a reason to, really. After my brother graduated from high school and continued on to college, I didn't see Monroe often, so there wasn't much of an opportunity to get to know her. Except for certain events, of course . . ."

"Events?"

"Oh, you know what I mean—as a Savannah native, I, fortunately, was born with the silver spoon, and attending societal functions is expected. I know most of the elite element . . ." Anna Lee grinned, breaking her staid façade. "But, only because I have to!"

Ryan laughed, playfully wagging his index finger at her. "You! You were toying with me, weren't you?"

"Of course! When you walked in my door, you looked like a fish out of water—and, I thought I'd have a little fun!"

The atmosphere relaxed into a comfort he only experienced with Colbie. Anna Lee was a gentle soul, and a bit devilish. Still, there was an ease about her—almost something he couldn't explain. "Okay—now that the fun and games are over . . ."

Anna Lee picked up her teacup. "Right. Well, the first time I met Agatha Culpepper was when Dobie—my brother—was home for college break. If I recall correctly, he and Monroe decided to get together and, much to Dobie's surprise, Agatha was sticking to Monroe like glue."

"What was your impression of her?"

"Spoiled rotten—there was no doubt by the look in her eye she considered Monroe quite a catch." She paused, recalling past decades. "And, he was—he could have had any girl, but he chose Agatha . . ."

"He didn't recognize her interest was his money?"

"Oh, that didn't matter—Agatha was bloody rich in her own right, and it seemed they made the perfect couple. He barely left her side, making it clear to anyone they were a force to be reckoned with . . ."

"A force?"

"Well, yes—Monroe Clyburn and Agatha Culpepper were allowed to do anything on campus they darned well pleased, and no one said a word."

Ryan noticed Anna Lee's lips tighten. "If you were several grades ahead of him, how is it you know so much about his campus life?"

"Because Buford kept me apprised about everything . . ."

"Buford Collins?"

Anna Lee nodded.

Ryan's expression didn't change at the mention of Collins. "How do you know Buford?"

"He and Dobie were best friends—but, Monroe and Agatha never gave him the time of day. He was beneath their class, and they didn't think much of his sister, either . . ."

"His sister?"

"Step-sister, actually—but, you'd never know it. He doted on her as if she were full bloodline. There were some who thought it disgusting—you, know . . . inappropriate. But, I never thought so—Buford wasn't the sharpest knife in the drawer, and I'm certain every penny he has now is due to the brains of those around him. I think he loved Gracie because she made him feel as if he were worth something."

She paused to take a sip of tea, then tucked an errant wisp of hair behind her ear. "Of course, when Gracie Brightwood wound up dead, Buford was the first person the authorities considered . . ."

"And?"

"Quickly dismissed. He was so distraught, he could barely see straight. Everyone knew there was no conceivable way he did it . . . "

"Murder?"

"Of course, it was—what else could it be?"

Ryan thought for a moment. "Gracie's name came up in our investigation, but we hit a brick wall—Beulah was the only one to mention it. She, too—according to my partner—thinks Gracie's death was murder, but that idea was swept quickly under the rug . . ."

"Beulah? Now there's a piece of work . . ."

"What do you mean? Colbie said she seemed nice enough . . ."

"Beulah Brightwood? Nice? She's as nasty as the day is long—and, never one to be trusted."

"I don't follow . . ."

"Ever since I've known her, she's been vengeful—especially when she discovered bitterness outweighs joy—or, at least, in her world. Ever since she lost Gracie, she turned into something uglier than she was before—and, I'm afraid, there were few of us who thought that wasn't possible!"

And, so, there they sat in the front room of Anna Lee's home as the sun turned in for the night, Ryan listening to Savannah's historian turn his and Colbie's investigation on it's ear. Finally, as he flipped up his coat collar to guard against the brisk, winter breeze, stepping onto the porch he felt compelled to turn without word to the woman who broke their case. Their eyes met, each knowing lives were about to change.

She was their connection.

CHAPTER

19

*D*ellinger and Baker stood at the foot of Agatha Clyburn's bed, trying not to stare. Before them lay a woman whose agony was etched in her face, eyes vacant and vacuous, no longer representing Savannah's highest society.

"Mrs. Clyburn?"

Nothing.

Dellinger tried again. "Mrs. Clyburn, I'm Detective Damion Dellinger, and this is Jonathan Baker—we need to ask you a few questions . . ."

Agatha's physician was by the door, standing sentinel should an 'issue' arise. Prior to granting Savannah's finest permission to interview her, they were warned—at the slightest indication of her being upset, they were to cease questioning.

They waited in silence, watching her eyelids flicker as if trying to wake herself from a deep coma. Dellinger glanced at the doctor. "Sedated?" When the doctor nodded, both detectives began to doubt she would ever be of help. Fractured beyond recognition, her ability to converse with anyone seemed impossible.

With everyone in the room watching intently, she stirred, then opened her eyes. "Mariska . . ."

Knowing her lucidity could be fleeting, Dellinger took immediate advantage. "What about Mariska, Mrs. Clyburn?"

Finally, she focused on the two men. "Dead . . ."

"We know, Mrs. Clyburn, and we're sorry for your loss. But, we're here to ask you about your husband . . ."

"Monroe?"

"Yes—that's right. Monroe—do you have any idea of who might want to cause him harm?"

Dellinger waited.

"Enemies . . ."

"What enemies, Mrs. Clyburn?"

"College . . ."

Dellinger didn't take his eyes from her. "He had enemies in college? Is that what you mean?"

She nodded.

Then, nothing more.

Ryan rapped on Colbie's hotel room door, hoping she were still awake. He hadn't kept in touch while at Anna Lee's, but he figured with what she told him? She needed to know, the sooner the better.

"Ryan?" Colbie peeked through the security peephole, laughing as she saw her partner making a silly face. Opening the door, she gave him the once over. "Just who I wanted to see—a twelve-year old!"

"I thought so!" He stepped across the threshold, then threw his jacket on the back of a chair. "You'll never guess who I just spent time with . . ."

"Well—we don't have specific interviews lined up until tomorrow . . . and, weren't you supposed to be taking a day off?"

"Yep—but, things didn't turn out that way . . ."

Tying her bathrobe, she plopped into the easy chair by the window. "Okay—shoot. What happened?"

By the time Colbie listened, asked a million questions, then considered the impact of Ryan's conversation with Anna Lee, she was more convinced the college Monroe and Agatha attended was the epicenter of their investigation. "Still," Ryan commented, "that doesn't do much good when it comes to finding out who murdered Mariska—only Monroe."

Colbie took a moment before answering. "Maybe. But, they're connected—I feel it."

"So—where do we go from here?"

"I think it's time we pay another call to Dean Beddington."

"Another surprise visit?"

"Of course—I can't imagine doing it any other way! Before we do that, however, I'd like to see if we can get face time with his wife . . . what's her name?"

"Mary Ellen—I checked right after you met with Beddington the first time."

Colbie grinned. "Excellent! I knew there was a reason I like having you around!"

The Beddington home was modest, although Colbie was certain they were living below their means. A brick paver walkway flanked by a well-manicured lawn led to an unassuming front door, nothing indicating those who dwelled within were held in high esteem in the small college town. "Are you sure this is it," she asked as Ryan checked the GPS one more time.

"Yep . . . right on the money!"

Colbie scanned the neighborhood as they sat in the car. "It's weird . . ."

"What's weird?"

"Well, don't you think someone who's the dean of a college would have something a little . . . more upscale?"

"Maybe they're not the upscale types . . ."

Colbie sat in silence, her intuitive senses in overdrive. "I don't know—there's something odd about this place. It's like it doesn't have any life to it . . ."

Ryan cut the engine. "Well, one thing's for sure—we're not going to find out anything if we keep sitting here!"

"You're right—let's check it out."

Within moments they stood at the front door, Colbie pressing the slightly rusted doorbell. "Do you hear anything," she asked as she turned, noticing a man across the street giving them the stink eye. "And, don't look now, but there's a guy watching every move we make . . ."

"Check . . ."

Colbie rang again. "I don't know, Ryan—I'm getting a weird feeling. I feel as if we're in the wrong place . . ." She glanced again at the man across the street, waving as if he were her best friend. "Excuse me," she called. "Is this where the Beddingtons live?"

The man glared at her. "Who wants to know?"

"I'm looking for Mary Ellen—I'm supposed to meet her here this morning . . ."

The man strode to his mailbox, then stood beside it, fully aware she didn't answer his question.

"There's no one home . . ."

Ryan watched him carefully. "I don't have a good feeling about his guy," he commented under his breath.

"I know—something's off."

Colbie waved, then started down the walk back to the car. "Thank you! I guess I must have the wrong day—or, something!" She flashed her best smile. "Thanks for your help!"

Satisfied, the man fetched his mail, then headed back to his garage as Colbie and Ryan climbed in the car. "That was weird," Ryan commented as he pulled away from the curb.

"It was . . . like he was guarding the home. You know—a watchman."

"I got the same feeling . . ."

"When I stood at the door, I also got the feeling no one lives there—no sense of energy. Or, anything, really . . ."

"You mean the Beddington's don't live there?"

"I'm not sure—maybe it's an old address." She glanced at him. "Are you sure it's the right one?"

Ryan nodded. "Yep—no other Ernest Beddingtons listed in the phone book, or in any library archives."

Colbie thought for a moment. "Then, why would they have a home listed in their name if they don't live there?"

"Maybe they rent it . . ."

"No—if someone lives there now, I would have felt it. There's always some sort of residual energy . . ."

"Okay—if that's the case, now what?"

"Let me think . . ." Colbie closed her eyes, allowing her intuition to guide her and, concentrating on Mary Ellen Beddington, it was a solid ten minutes before she was ready to surface from her intuitive mind.

Ryan glanced at her. "Well?"

"Let's head to the college . . ."

Beulah stared at Morgan, the only thing between them a cottage screen door in need of repair. "What are you doing here?"

"Oh, I think you know . . ."

"No, I don't. Our agreement was we were to never lay eyes on each other again . . ."

"Yes—but, circumstances change. Now, are you going to stand there looking like you got caught with your pants down, or are you going to invite me in?"

Beulah hesitated, finally opening the door. "Did anyone see you?"

"Don't be a fool, Beulah—if I were being tailed, I'd know it!"

"Oh, I don't know—from what I hear, you've been off your game lately, Morgan. Age, perhaps?"

Morgan's eyes filled with scalding animosity. "I'd tread lightly, if I were you. You seem to forget who's calling the shots . . ."

No words passed between them as Morgan made herself comfortable in Beulah's favorite chair—an intended sleight. "I assume you heard . . . "

"Of course—it was plastered all over the news."

For twenty minutes the two women sat across from each other, discussing a kink in the plan. "Her name is Colbie Colleen—her sidekick's name is Ryan," Morgan stated.

"How do you know?"

"That doesn't make any difference—the question is what are we going to do about it?"

For the first time, Beulah Brightwood connected with her spine. She rose, then headed for the front door. "I'll handle her," she promised, looking squarely at the woman whom everyone feared. "The more important aspect of our conversation is we no longer need your services . . ."

"Excuse me?"

Beulah opened the door. "You heard me. And, one more thing, Morgan. Perhaps it will be wise if you fully understand who's really calling the shots . . ."

"Did you check the call records?"

"Yep—only two that evening. One after midnight . . ."

"From?"

"The first one was from someone named Cassius Sprague, and that call logged at precisely six forty-seven . . ."

Detective Dellinger sat back in his chair, twirling his pencil like a mini baton. "I've heard that name—what do you know?"

"Sprague is a high roller in the pharmaceutical industry, and Clyburn's staunch competitor. I talked to a couple of people, and it was pretty clear they despised each other, yet social protocol dictated an outwardly civil appearance."

"Sprague called twice?"

Detective Baker shook his head. "Nope—it seems he dialed Clyburn's cell, but disconnected immediately after the call went through . . ."

Dellinger continued twirling his pencil. "Who was the other one?"

Baker chuckled. "It's a good thing you're sitting down because you're going to love this. . ."

"I'll decide what I'm going to love . . "

Baker grinned. "Beddington."

"No shit? Ernest Beddington?"

"Not quite . . ."

"What do you mean, 'not quite?'"

"The call registered after midnight wasn't from Ernest Beddington's cell or land line . . ."

"Knock off the suspense bullshit, Baker—who the hell called Clyburn?"

Baker grinned. "Beddington's wife."

Both were silent for several seconds, thinking about who linked to who, and why, Dellinger finally making his decision. "We need to talk to Colbie Colleen . . ."

CHAPTER

20

The young woman behind the desk instantly recognized Colbie from her first visit. Dean Beddington made it clear if she showed up again, he was unavailable. "Dean Beddington isn't in, I'm afraid . . ."

"Oh, my—that's too bad! I know I should have called, but I wanted to deliver the good news in person . . ."

Beddington's assistant flinched slightly. "Good news? Is there anything I can tell him when he gets back?"

Colbie smiled. "I'm afraid not—but, if you'll please tell him it has to do with my visit awhile ago . . ."

"I'll be glad to . . ."

"When do you expect him?"

"He didn't say—it's anyone's guess when we have campus guests . . ."

"I understand—I know he's incredibly busy." She paused purposely. "Well, if you hear from him, will you please ask him to call me?"

"Of course . . ."

Colbie slipped her hand into her coat pocket. "Here's my card—and, the sooner the better. I think he's going to like what I have to tell him!"

"I will!" Beddington's assistant smiled, thrilled with the thought of giving the dean good news for once. Lately, things hadn't been going too well—her boss was edgy, and never in a good mood.

Ryan smiled, impressed at Colbie's natural ability to weave any situation in the direction she wished it to go. "Well, thank you! You know how to reach us!"

With that they left, leaving the young woman with thoughts of calling Beddington to let him know who stopped by.

"Pretty smooth," Ryan commented, as they reached the car. "Telling her you have good news was a stroke of genius!"

"She's young, and gullible—my guess is she called Beddington the second we walked out the door . . ."

"Probably—now what?"

"We wait . . ."

Nearly a year passed since their last conversation at the golf club, the topic of discussion Mariska Clyburn's unfortunate and untimely passing. Of course, much happened during that time, and no one would have guessed Monroe would be murdered, or his wife committed to the state's finest psychiatric hospital—the 'loony bin' as many called it after hearing of her complete mental fracturing.

Cassius Sprague swirled expensive scotch in its glass, contemplating recent events. "There is, of course, speculation about Clyburn Pharmaceuticals—it seems those left to right the ship are the boys . . ."

"Those Clyburn boys don't know their asses from a hole in the ground . . ." Buford Collins took an aggressive sip, his fingers looking pudgier than they had the last time they met. "It might be the right time . . ."

"The right time for what? A buyout?"

"Perhaps . . ."

Sprague managed a smug grin—the last thing he wanted was to be in league with Collins. "You can bet the Clyburn boys aren't going to let go—the company is all they have. It's their rightful silver spoon . . ." He thought for a moment. "Besides, you can bet the cops are all over every aspect of Monroe's life, and I don't want any part of it."

"Have they contacted you?"

"The cops? No—but, it's only a matter of time before they weasel their way in to anyone's life who had something to do with Monroe—personally, or his business."

Buford nodded. "Of course, there's his wife—I wonder what she knew before going off the deep end . . ."

It wasn't actually a question—more of a private musing, but, it was enough for Sprague's thoughts to spring to attention. "Knew about what . . ."

"Oh, come on, Cassius—it's no secret Monroe had a taste for the ladies. Ever since college, really . . ."

"Perhaps, but I don't see what that has to do with anything . . ."

"Maybe nothing—but, you know the fury of a woman scorned."

Sprague put his glass on the table. "Are you saying you think Agatha murdered Clyburn because he was unfaithful? C'mon—I know for a fact she loved Monroe. If not for his shining personality, then for his money—she always had it, and losing her safety net wasn't on her list of things to do."

"What about what happened at college?"

"What about it? Every guy cheats on his girlfriend at some time or another—if it's available, why not?"

Buford bristled at Sprague's nonchalance. "It was a little more than cheating, as I remember it . . ."

"Even it were, I don't see what that has to do with Monroe's murder . . ."

"There's no denying Agatha went into a downward spiral when she heard about it. All I'm saying is if Monroe didn't change his ways, I'm guessing Agatha still has it in her to wield her wrath . . ."

Cassius thought about Buford's hypothesis, finally giving credence to the possibility. "What was the name of that girl?"

"What girl?"

"In college—Agatha was considered a suspect for a while, I think . . ."

"Gracie . . ."

Sprague smiled, and nodded. "Ah, yes—Gracie Brightwood. I completely forgot she was related to you! No wonder you're thinking about the possibility of Agatha's offing Monroe—after all, if she did it before, she could do it again. Is that the basis for your thinking?"

"Precisely."

His voice was barely a whisper.

Two hours into their surveillance, Colbie's cell buzzed. "It's Dellinger . . ." She waited for three impatient buzzes before answering. "Colbie."

"It's Dellinger. Where are you?"

"At the college . . ."

"To see Beddington?"

Colbie picked up on the impatience in his voice. "What's going on, Detective? And, yes—we're here to see Beddington." She tapped the speaker icon, so Ryan could listen.

For the next few minutes they were quiet as the detective brought her up to speed about the cell phone calls, their location, and, finally, the news it was Mary Ellen Beddington who placed the last call to Monroe Clyburn.

She glanced at Ryan. "Since we're here, we'll pick up on Beddington's wife . . ."

"Excellent—we're moving forward on our questioning outside of Clyburn's close circle to business associates and colleagues."

"Including Buford Collins?"

"Especially Collins—if he's involved in either Mariska's or her father's death, we've given him enough time to feel comfortable . . ."

"But, it's only been a few days . . ."

"That's what I said—he's had enough time."

Moments later, they clicked off, Colbie writing notes on a small notepad. "It's getting late—let's plan on staying here tonight, and we can pick up in the morning." She paused. "Or, better yet—let's check in, then see if we can tail Beddington to his real home."

"Good thought, but what if he doesn't come back to his office?"

Colbie grinned, closing the notepad. "Oh, he will . . ."

There was one thing Morgan Stratford was clear about when she walked down Beulah Brightwood's porch steps—she'd been used. Knowing that had nothing to do with intuition—it was a cold fact to which she chose to be blind for the last two years. Allowing Beulah to manipulate her was, in itself, embarrassing—but, to be wittingly complicit with no possibility of reward? Unconscionable. And, it was a situation calling for only one thing . . .

Revenge.

She sat quietly at her small table, holding the cards in her hands. In her thoughts, she called on those who passed over for help as she laid them in her favorite, familiar spread—asking no question, she allowed the card's energies to provide what she needed to know.

Closing her eyes, she instantly tapped into the one person who could disrupt everything. *She's strong*, she thought, as she recognized Colbie's intuition. Then, another realization. *She's stronger than I . . .*

In her mind's eye, she watched as Colbie began to unravel the truth, her energy and commitment far stronger than Morgan's. By the end of her meditation, the psychic to Savannah's socialites was faced with answering the most pressing question—should she get out, or see it through?

It was a choice she wasn't yet prepared to make.

Colbie and Ryan staked out Beddington's office with nothing to show for it—something Ryan found necessary to point out. "You said," he mentioned in his most serious tone, "Beddington would show up . . ."

"Hey! I can be wrong!" She laughed as she pulled a packaged salad from the delivery bag. "This one's yours—but, they only gave you one dressing."

"What? I asked for two!"

She laughed, extracting her own salad. "Oh, well—too bad for you! Oh, gee—lookie here! I have two dressings!"

He couldn't help but grin. Ever since he'd known her, she loved twisting the knife, teasing him with certain affection. "So—we bolt our food. Then what?"

"I've been thinking about that . . ." She checked her watch. "I recall Beddington mentioning he specialized in poetry when getting his degrees . . ."

"So? I remember—I thought majoring in poetry was a little weird . . ."

"He didn't major in it—but, he does have a particular interest. So, that makes me wonder where he might spend a great deal of his time . . ."

Ryan placed the plastic lid on the dressing container, licking off the dribbles on his fingers. "I don't know—where does a nerd spend his time?"

"The library . . ."

"Ah! Good point!"

"Let's check in at the hotel, then take a stroll around the campus . . ."

"I don't have any idea where the library is . . ."

"Neither do I, but that's not the point—it's about what or whom we see on the way there."

Ryan shook his head. "I don't get it—if we're looking for Beddington at the library, isn't that the point?"

"Yes, but think about what we can learn on the way there. It's a Friday night, and kids are going to be out and about . . ."

Ryan tried spreading petrified butter on his dinner roll, ripping the top completely. "Just once I'd like to get soft butter from a restaurant—and, I'm still going to be hungry."

"We can grab a bite—so, after we're done, let's head out. I have a feeling we won't come up empty-handed . . ."

Mario's Pizza was in full swing, college students in and out as they went on their way to a typical weekend evening. "I think there's a Mario's Pizza in every town on the planet,"

Ryan commented as they looked for a table. Students lined the bar, lifting beers at the very notion of a toast, a few three sheets to the wind even though it was before nine.

Colbie grabbed his sleeve. "There's a table!"

Winding through the crowd, they were lucky enough to snag one in the back, away from raucous noise and spilled beer. "The gods are with us," Colbie commented as Ryan pulled out her chair. "I'll bet this place is packed all night . . ."

"No doubt—I remember when I was in college. This isn't all that different . . ."

"You remember back that far?"

"Funny . . . do you want something to eat?"

"Yes! I'm with you—that salad wasn't nearly enough!"

Ryan scanned the room, noting there were no other empty tables. "I'm surprised they allowed us to stay at a table for four with so many people here . . ."

Both watched the crowd, a young couple approaching them just as Colbie's and Ryan's pizza arrived. "Do you mind if we sit with you," the young woman asked. "I promise not to bother you!"

Colbie smiled. "Of course!"

Ryan wasn't feeling so generous.

"Please—have a seat!"

The girl gushed thanks as they pulled out chairs, and took off their coats. "It's never this busy! I'm Natalie—Nat, for short—and, this is Andy."

Colbie returned the intros. "We're pleased to meet both

of you! What's the special occasion?"

"I don't know—there probably isn't one. Just a bunch of kids wanting to get drunk!"

"But, not you?"

Her boyfriend laughed. "If only you knew—no, we're not the drinking types. We're just hungry!"

For the next thirty minutes, they got to know each other, Colbie impressed with the couple's maturity, and good manners.

Timing was perfect.

"So—what are you two majoring in?" Colbie added a small bit of Parmesan cheese to her slice, acting as if theirs were a normal 'stranger-meets-stranger' conversation.

Nat's eyes lit up. "English! I love it—especially poetry!"

"Really? I loved English when I was in school—but, I took a different route."

Ryan's turn. "Didn't I read somewhere Dean . . ." He glanced at Colbie. "What's his name?"

Nat couldn't contain her excitement—having someone to talk to about her passion didn't come along often, and she intended to make the most of it. "Beddington!"

Before Ryan could answer, Colbie maneuvered the conversation where she wanted it to go. "That's it! What's he like?" Colbie turned her full attention to the two students. "I imagine he's pretty tough . . ."

"He's not bad—I don't have him for any of my classes because he's strictly for upper level courses."

Colbie nodded. "That makes sense—when I was in school, grad students taught some entry-level courses, and the great profs were for juniors and seniors . . ." She took a bite, then swallowed. "What made you choose this school? The English department?"

Nat glanced at Andy, blushing. "No—I followed Andy." Embarrassed, she immediately felt as if she had to explain. "I didn't know what I wanted to do, so . . ."

"I get it—what about now? Was it the right choice?"

"Kind of—although it wasn't a burning desire at the time, I discovered I love figuring things out . . ."

Colbie focused on the young woman sitting next to Ryan. "Not sure I follow . . ."

"Well, Dean Beddington was a 'guest' lecturer at a book store in the Savannah Starland District in my sophomore year, and I decided to go with a couple of friends . . ."

"What was the lecture about?"

"Well, it wasn't what I expected, that's for sure!"

Colbie's eyebrows arched. "What did you expect?"

"Not that! It was about murder mysteries!"

"Murder mysteries in general, or do you mean he writes them?"

"He writes them! And, at that time, I was considering majoring in creative writing—so, I figured why not? I stayed!"

Ryan's turn. "What about your interest in poetry?"

"Oh, that wasn't until recently . . ."

Colbie glanced at Ryan. "Have you read any of his books? Are they available on Amazon?"

Nat shook her head. "No—he said he's still working on his first. He wants it to be perfect before it goes on the market . . ."

Ryan listened closely as Colbie extracted information from the lovely Natalie, who remained clueless about being grilled by a professional. It was masterful, really—and, for the next two hours, they talked about English. Dean Beddington.

What comprised a perfect murder.

CHAPTER

21

*D*etective Dellinger extended his hand. "Thank you for coming down to speak with us, Mr. Sprague. I promise I won't keep you long . . ."

Cassius Sprague determined quickly it wasn't the right time to show his outward displeasure at being summoned for questioning regarding Monroe Clyburn's murder. "Quite understandable, Detective—private pharmaceuticals is a small niche, and it's prudent to speak to everyone."

Within moments, Detective Dellinger sat across from Sprague, opting for an interview in his office rather than an interrogation room. "Not so intimidating," he commented to

Baker before Sprague arrived. "And, it shows respect for his position in society . . ."

"What a bunch of bullshit . . ." Baker was always of the opinion high society didn't mean crap.

Dellinger, however, knew better. "That may be—but, it's necessary bullshit."

Cassius decided to give immediate control of the conversation a try. "So, Detective—what do you need to know?"

Dellinger focused on his notes. "It says here . . ."

"Here?"

"Sorry—a habit I picked up from my mother when I was six." He looked up, smiling. "It's strange the things we bring with us from our younger years, isn't it?"

Sprague wasn't sure if the question were rhetorical, but, there was something in the detective's tone signaling it wasn't. "I believe we're fools when we're young—all of us making mistakes we wish never would have happened . . ."

Interesting . . . Dellinger took note. "Well, let's get down to the reason you're here. It's no secret you were in Monroe's private circle, Mr. Sprague . . ."

"Private circle? Hardly, Detective . . . it's no secret we tolerated each other, and that's about it. Purely professional obligation . . ."

"So, you didn't call him on the night of his murder—February seventeenth?"

Let the tap dancing begin. "I spoke with Monroe regarding business a couple of weeks ago, but I don't recall the exact date . . ."

"It says here . . ." Again, he looked up, grinning. "Sorry—what kind of business, Mr. Sprague?"

"The market, mostly . . ." Sprague met Dellinger's gaze with his own. "Nothing nefarious, I assure you . . ."

Momentary silence—just long enough for Dellinger to recognize how quickly Cassius Sprague became infinitely more uncomfortable. "Who do you think murdered Monroe Clyburn, Mr. Sprague?"

Cassius didn't flinch. "You're sure it was murder? I hadn't heard—officially."

"No one has . . ."

Sprague sat, each moment offering nothing but dramatic silence. "Have you spoken to Buford Collins?"

There it was—the deflection. Otherwise known as throwing someone under the bus.

"Not yet . . ."

Baker leaned up against the only file cabinet in Dellinger's office. "Why do you mention him?"

"There was always bad blood between them, although they kept it to themselves . . ."

"How do you know of it?"

"About a year ago I was chatting with Buford at the golf club. He didn't say anything in particular—it was a feeling I got when he mentioned Clyburn's name . . ."

Then? The bombshell.

"After Mariska Clyburn left my company," Cassius continued, "I carried on her cell degeneration research, knowing I could corner the private market before Clyburn had the chance. No one was to know, but, somehow, Collins got wind of it. By the time we parted ways at the golf club, he was all for someone making Monroe Clyburn's life a living hell—and, he threatened to blackmail me if I didn't comply."

Dellinger waited, knowing instinctively Sprague had more to say.

"So, I called him on it—I asked him why he wanted to see Monroe Clyburn lose it all if, indeed, that would ever be possible. Personally, I doubt it . . ."

"What did he say?"

Cassius Sprague glanced at Baker, then focused on Dellinger. "Payback, Detective. That's all he said . . . payback."

By the time they made it back to their hotel, Colbie and Ryan were exhausted. Tailing Beddington hit the back burner when they learned about his propensity for a good mystery, and that meant spending as much time as possible with their newfound college friends. "Does that mean," Colbie pondered as they treated themselves to a nightcap, "he wrote something, and wanted to see if he could carry it out?"

Ryan shook his head. "I don't think so—besides, that seems the obvious conclusion. Very Grade B—and, I don't think Beddington is a Grade B kind of guy . . ."

It wasn't often Ryan and Colbie weren't on the same page, but he felt strongly there was something else at work. "Wanna know what I think?" He put his drink down, giving her his complete attention.

"Maybe . . ."

"I think Ernest Beddington doesn't have anything to do with anything—the stranger's phone call whispering a clue? A poem? Rather suspect, don't you think?"

"Well . . ."

"Think about it! It was corny, if nothing else! If this guy is into writing mysteries, when we showed up on his doorstep, he figured it was the best time to test his plot . . ."

Colbie thought for a moment. "If that's the case, Beddington is quite capable of Grade B . . ."

Ryan leaned his head on the back of the couch, staring at the ceiling. "You're right . . . damn!"

"So—what are you saying? We bag Ernest Beddington, altogether? What about his wife? The cell phone record to Clyburn's phone—how do you explain that?"

"I haven't figured that out yet . . ."

Colbie was quiet for several minutes, thinking. "So, you're saying we fell for a red herring. In a way, we were his accidental audience . . ."

"Yep."

In silence, a minute passed. "I don't know, but I'm not

ready to eighty-six Beddington. There's something . . ."

"If he knew him—even if the caller *were* Monroe—that doesn't mean Beddington's a murderer! I didn't want to say anything until I was sure, but when Nat said he was into writing mysteries, everything fell into place as far as he's concerned. At least, for me, it did . . ."

"That means if Beddington isn't involved—or, his wife— we go back to the main reason I'm in Savannah in the first place. Monroe Clyburn . . ."

"And, his daughter's murder . . ."

"Exactly."

"Do you think they're related?"

Colbie nodded. "Maybe—remember when I said the main players in all of this are Collins, Beulah, and Beddington?" She paused. "The more I think about it, the more your theory makes sense—maybe we switch Beddington for Morgan."

"So, Beddington is off of our list?"

"Not completely . . ."

Ryan didn't head for his own room until after midnight. For the first time in weeks, they felt energized, knowing they were going in the right direction. It wasn't until Colbie felt a strange presence did the topic of conversation change—it was only for a moment, but there was no mistake.

As Ryan laid out flow chart of suspects, Colbie's intuitive mind leapt to life, flooding her with dark, sinister images. Again, she saw two people—definitely women—wet, with straggly hair. But, there was something different from her first vision. That night? A third person, cloaked in black, entered the scene to stand with them. Then, with executed precision, the third figure turned, sending dark, toxic energy into Colbie's mind's eye.

" . . . don't you think so?" Ryan waited. "Colbie?" He turned, expecting her to be asleep in her chair—what he witnessed was something of which he would never speak to anyone outside of that room.

She sat, staring, her body completely still—suddenly, she turned to Ryan, her eyes vacant. Black. A frigid chill swept past him as he felt the tender stroke of icy fingers against his face. "What the . . . Colbie!"

But, there was more.

The stench of rotting, fetid flesh choked the room as if a warning of what's to come. "Colbie!" Ryan gagged as he tried to get to her, only to be blocked by something he couldn't see.

Again, he called to her, his voice stern and sharp. "Colbie! Colbie!"

Then, it was over.

Colbie's expression changed as warmth filled the air, and he watched as she tried to make sense of what happened.

"What do you remember," he asked, taking her trembling hand in his. Her fear was palpable and, for the first time, he wondered if her abilities were worth the trouble. What he witnessed was something new. Different.

And, it scared him. "Colbie?"

She could barely speak. "Morgan . . ."

CHAPTER

22

Detective Dellinger listened as Colbie and Ryan recounted their time at the university, meeting Nat and Andy, and Ryan's belief Beddington was a red herring, perhaps of their own making. Both, however, thought it best not to mention Colbie's psychic connection with Morgan Stratford—doing so could lead down a lane they didn't want to travel.

"It seems we wasted a lot of time . . ." Baker didn't bother to veil his distaste for the woman sitting in his boss's office. He didn't give a whit about her talents, or supposed abilities—if they didn't yield results, what the hell good were they?

Dellinger's indulging her didn't help.

"I'm not completely convinced Beddington's off the radar," Colbie explained. "I still believe he knows something. But, do I believe he's responsible for Monroe's murder? No—there's something else at work . . ." Colbie paused, waiting for a response. Any response.

Nothing.

"So, in light of that, Ryan and I are focusing our attention on three people . . ."

Dellinger gave no indication he was going to follow suit. "And, those people are . . ."

"Almost the same—Buford Collins, Beulah Brightwood, and Morgan Stratford. As I said, like before, but switching Beddington for the psychic.

"Why them? Just to refresh my memory . . ."

"Because this is about revenge. The question is what do Collins, Beulah, and Morgan have in common . . ."

"And?"

Colbie hesitated a moment. "The murder of Gracie Brightwood, Detective . . ."

Morgan Stratford was an odd child, well into single digits when she realized she was different from other kids on the playground. By the time she hit the ripe old age of thirteen, she embraced her oddities. By adulthood?

A way of life.

Most of her younger years were spent with a solitary friend—maybe two—but certainly no more. Talking about people whom others couldn't see put a damper on long-term relationships with the occasional exception of an outer edge group of teens dabbling in the dark arts. Predictably, it was among them she felt most comfortable, forging alliances with outcasts and fringe elements of Savannah's occult society.

Still, with everything against her as far as acceptance by 'normal' people, she managed solidifying a slot among Savannah's highest echelon. Private readings were most lucrative, padding her pocket with hundreds instead of singles and, of course, her client list remained private. But, a few leaked their association with her, prompting secret conversations among their friends.

Then, they made appointments.

So, when Buford Collins stepped into her private reading room for the first time, she smelled money before he had a chance to take a seat. By the time he left, weekly appointments for the next month were on his personal docket, knowing he finally found the help he so desperately needed.

And, he wasn't the only one. Agatha Clyburn commissioned her services, but only if she arrived through the back entrance so not to be seen by 'attentive' neighbors. Marcus and Melbourne were regulars, too, although Marcus thought she was as fake as her eyelashes. But, he indulged his mother, promising secrecy as far as Monroe was concerned. "He'll say it's a bunch of hogwash," she confided to her son one day. "But, I know better . . ."

Colbie knew better, too.

Two months after Monroe's murder, Dellinger and Baker sat in Buford's office, waiting for an answer. "Well, Mr. Collins? Where were you the night of February seventeenth?"

At first glance, one might think Buford was handling the detective's questioning with an admirable degree of aplomb—except for the beads of sweat forming just south of his hairline. "I don't know—I guess I was home."

"You guess?"

"Look at me—I'm not exactly what you call a good catch! Where the hell else would I be?"

Dellinger watched as a single droplet of sweat inched its way down to Buford's brow. "I'm sure I have no idea, Mr. Collins . . ." He referred to his notes. "What's your relationship with Beulah Brightwood?"

Buford's left eye twitched. "Beulah? Why do you want to know about her?"

"Please answer the question . . ."

"She's my step-sister."

"And, Morgan Stratford?"

"Morgan—a relationship? Not exactly—I see her for personal . . . guidance."

The air felt thick—heavy—as Dellinger ticked off his questions. Finally, the question he knew would more than ruffle Buford's resolve. "Tell me about Gracie . . ."

And, that's when Buford Collins called time. "I demand the right to counsel . . ."

It was a proclamation carrying little surprise.

Trying to make sense of their case, Colbie sat in a booth in the restaurant tavern, her fingers gracefully holding a glass of merlot. Traffic turned out to be a nightmare, so Ryan wasn't certain he could arrive within the hour—until then, she was on her own.

"Do you mind if I join you?" Detective Dellinger stood beside her table, offering an engaging smile. "I don't mean to intrude . . ."

Colbie grinned, motioning for him to sit. "You're not—I was thinking about the case, I'm afraid . . ."

"Where's your sidekick?"

"Stuck in traffic—we're supposed to meet here, but my gut tells me he's not going to make it."

Dellinger glanced at two menus scooted to the back end of the table, leaning against the wall. "Did you order?"

Colbie shook her head, then took a sip.

"Then, how about dinner with me?"

"I'm afraid I might not be good company—I'll be honest, this case has me baffled. I know I'm missing something right in front of my face . . ."

"A beautiful face, I might add . . ."

Colbie blushed, enjoying the compliment—it sparked a slight tingle she hadn't felt for quite some time.

"Excuse me, please . . ." She glanced at her phone, then answered. A few seconds later, she clicked off. "Ryan—he'll meet me back at the hotel."

"Then, you need to eat . . ."

So, for the next two hours they chatted and laughed, each enjoying their time away from the job. Sometime at the beginning of hour two, the detective confessed he was intrigued by her abilities, asking myriad questions about how they worked.

"Well, it's something I've had since childhood, and I'm not sure I can explain it. Sometimes—most times—it's like watching a movie in my mind. Those visions usually lead me in the right direction when I'm involved in a case . . ."

Although he didn't understand completely, there was something about her that made sense. She tried to explain, finally agreeing to table the conversation until another time.

"Do you head back to the West Coast after you wrap up your case here," he asked as he picked up the tab, and they headed for the door.

"Probably—I haven't decided. Why?"

He smiled, placing his palm at the small of her back, escorting her as a gentleman would. "Just wondering . . ."

CHAPTER

23

Buford sat, his eyes belying everything was just as it should be. Since his conversation with Dellinger and Baker, sleep proved elusive as he tried to figure out the best way to get the hell out of Dodge. Dellinger's request that he not leave town was more than disconcerting—it was enough to drive him completely around the bend, and his gut told him he was on the brink of living his life behind bars. A thought he didn't take lightly.

His stubby legs barely touched the floor as he sat on the side of his bed, shoulders sagging under unthinkable weight.

Despite Morgan's assurances everything would be okay, he had the feeling he couldn't trust her lately—and, that was definitely a precarious situation. So, he had a decision to make—call Dellinger, tell the truth, and let the chips fall, or go on the lam? Finally, he crawled under the covers, his mind tracing every second—every event—recalling that night in February so many years ago.

It was colder than usual—one of Savannah's cold snaps having everyone talking for a couple of days, and then it was back to business as usual. He hadn't heard from Gracie, but, given the fact she was a homebody, he was certain she was staying warm in her dorm. Of course, there were no cell phones back then, so the only way he had to contact her was by calling the dormitory receptionist, asking her to let Gracie know she had a call. Usually, it was such a laborious process, they waited until the weekends to be in touch.

It wasn't until the authorities wound up on his doorstep did he learn the heart shattering, agonizing news—Gracie was found caught up in spindly branches, face down in the river outside of town, her body swollen in death. "Was it an accident," he asked, but authorities said he needed to answer a few questions at the precinct. With barely time to put on a jacket, they whisked him downtown, into the precinct through a back door, then into an interrogation room.

At that time, he didn't know enough about police tactics, so calling an attorney didn't enter his mind—and, it was that situation prompting his immediate request for counsel when Dellinger questioned him. It was a mistake he refused to make a second time.

Tears streamed as Buford thought of Gracie. *Accused of her murder? How could they? They didn't know at the time of my questioning if she died at the hands of someone—their approach was nothing but political conjecture, and the cops were directed by state officials to make it snappy . . .*

That made sense, of course, because there was an upcoming election—it certainly wouldn't look good to have a college student's unsolved murder on their hands. Back then, it was an uncommon situation—one to be taken seriously, and without hesitation.

But, by the time he was hauled in a second time, there was no question of Buford's innocence—he was too much of a wreck at the mere mention of Gracie's name to seriously consider him a suspect. Besides, as days passed, her death was chalked up to an unfortunate accident, and any mention of Gracie Brightwood lasted for only a couple of months, at best.

Beulah, however, refused to let the death of her sister slide unceremoniously into a cold case file, vowing to find the person who murdered her. It was she—not Buford—who first contacted Morgan Stratford. And, it wasn't to take advantage of the psychic's knowledge of the dark arts—only to seek advice about who should be held responsible. It was during her readings, Morgan revealed Gracie's death was, indeed, the result of foul play.

Pinpointing by whom was the tricky part . . .

"Is this it?" Dellinger glanced at Baker as he pulled off the main road onto an obscure lane, overgrown bushes eclipsing the view of everything but what was in front of them.

"I think so . . ."

"Colbie said it would be difficult to see—so, I'm guessing this is right . . ."

Baker shot him a look. He didn't know what his partner saw in her, but, clearly, it was something. "There!"

They pulled into a clearing, a small cottage with an inviting porch suddenly in front of them. Dellinger scanned the yard, noticing a tiny work shed at the rear of the house. "This definitely is it . . ."

As they approached the porch, Beulah greeted them in much the same way she welcomed Colbie and Ryan. "Can I help you," she asked as they climbed the steps.

Dellinger showed his badge, Baker following suit. "Detectives Dellinger and Baker. I'd like to talk to you about Gracie Brightwood . . ."

"Gracie?"

"Yes, Ma'am . . ."

It was clear they weren't going away, so there was no other choice. "Please, come in . . ."

After displaying usual southern hospitality, Beulah settled into her favorite chair. "Now, what about Gracie?"

Dellinger thought he noticed a slight change in demeanor when she asked her question, as if bracing herself for a verbal onslaught. "According to records, the cause of death was an accident—but, I'd like to hear your thoughts, if you don't mind . . ."

Beulah remained silent for several seconds, then focused her undivided attention on Dellinger. "It so happens, I do mind, Detective. I see no reason to dredge up the past . . ."

"I understand it will be painful, Ms. Brightwood—but, unfortunately, you have no option. You can either talk to us here, or downtown." He glanced at Baker. "We're good either way . . ."

"I see—well, what is it you want to know about Gracie, Detective?"

"I understand you think her death wasn't accidental—it was murder. Is that correct?"

Beulah straightened in her chair. "It was murder, sure as I'm sittin' here—why would Gracie be out on a cold night, down by the river? I'll tell you why, Detective—she wouldn't! Gracie hated cold weather, and avoided it at all costs." She paused. "In fact, that's why she chose to stay in Georgia for her college education when she had a scholarship up north!"

"You mentioned that to the authorities, I assume . . ."

"Of course, I did, but they didn't want to hear it! At first, they set their sights on Buford—but, anyone could look at him, and see that wasn't the case. He was destroyed . . ."

Dellinger nodded. "Tell me about Buford's relationship with Gracie—I understand they were close."

"Oh, yes—people didn't understand it, either. Said there was something going on—something ugly. But, nothing could have been further from the truth—Gracie saw something in Buford that no one else saw. When Buford's father married our mother, Gracie took to Buford instantly . . ."

"In what way?"

Beulah smiled. "You've seen Buford, Detective—he's not exactly known as a lady's man. But, Gracie didn't care about that—she was always telling him he could be anything he wanted to be. 'It's your world,' she would say . . ." She paused, recalling the memory. "And, Buford believed her—she was his champion, no matter the cause."

A tinge of sadness filled the room as she continued. "So, when that was taken away from Buford . . . well, his life took a different turn."

"How so?"

"He retreated into himself—finally, he left school because he couldn't bear the thought of continuing without Gracie to urge him on . . ."

Dellinger watched Beulah carefully. *She's good*, he thought, wondering if Baker were as appreciative of her fine performance.

Time for a shift. "How do you know Morgan Stratford? She's a psychic, is she not?"

As the words left his mouth, Beulah's face set. "You know she's a psychic, Detective—please don't insult my intelligence." She paused. "Morgan Stratford helped Buford after Gracie's murder . . ."

"How?"

Beulah's eyes narrowed. "Because she, too, thought Gracie's death wasn't an accident—and, he was hoping she could identify Gracie's murderer."

"She could see that?"

"In her Tarot cards—yes. She said she could . . ."

"Did you believe her?"

"Yes, Detective, I did."

"Did she? Reveal the murderer, I mean . . ."

Beulah looked down, brushing imaginary crumbs from her lap. "Yes."

Dellinger glanced at Baker who was watching every move. "Who does she think murdered Gracie?"

Her eyes met his. "Agatha Culpepper. It was Agatha Culpepper who murdered my sister!" By design, she failed to mention it was she who first contacted Morgan Stratford.

Just in case it made a difference . . .

Colbie and Ryan listened on the cell's speaker as Detective Dellinger filled them in on his interview with Beulah Brightwood. "Agatha? I don't know, Damion . . ."

Ryan winced at the familiarity. "Did she say why," he asked.

"At first, her story seemed to be based on the emotion of losing her sister. But, when she started to explain . . ."

"It made sense?" Ryan glanced at Colbie. "Do you think she's right?"

Colbie didn't wait for his answer. "It does make sense. Remember when I said all of this was about revenge? I think that's exactly the case . . . but, we still have to figure how everything goes together."

"Agreed. At least we know we're heading in the right direction . . ." Detective Dellinger hesitated, unsure of broaching his idea with them. "You also said Morgan Stratford was part of the equation—and, she's the only one we haven't interviewed."

Ryan had a feeling he knew what was coming. "And?"

Dellinger cleared his throat. "Well, I think you, Colbie, are the one to conduct that interview. You're going to know if she's full of shit, or if she's the real deal . . ."

Colbie nodded, even though he couldn't see her. "I agree—that makes the most sense."

"But, haven't we assumed she's the real deal?" Ryan focused on Colbie. "You said she's strong—that sounds like the real deal, to me!"

Colbie smiled, touched by his wanting to keep her out of harm's way. "She's nothing I can't handle . . ."

"Then it's set? You'll interview her—I can haul her in, or you can see what you can get out of her at her place."

Ryan nodded. "At least I know exactly where that is!"

After briefly discussing a strategy, Dellinger rang off, leaving Colbie and Ryan to themselves. "Things are happening," Ryan commented.

"Yep. We need to be ready . . ."

Agatha Clyburn sat in a chair, looking out the window, thinking about Monroe. Mariska.

Her life.

How she wound up in such a position, she didn't know. It was no secret she was emotionally fragile throughout her life, but she never imagined being without her ability to navigate difficult times. But, there she was—feeble, fractured, and friendless.

Then, her thoughts turned to Gracie Brightwood.

The little trollop, she remembered as she watched raindrops splat on the thick glass, recalling when she learned of the dalliance with her boyfriend. It had, apparently, been going on for some time under her nose—a situation making her look foolish.

A situation she wouldn't tolerate.

Getting Gracie out of the dorm wasn't easy, and Agatha considered it a personal victory when she agreed to meet her at a local coffee shop. Promising she had something to tell, Gracie took the bait, never suspecting ill will.

That night, there was a chill. An uncustomary dusting of snow laced with imperceptible ice crunched beneath their feet as they strolled the river's edge, talking about everything—school and Monroe, in particular. Agatha confessed her suspicions about Monroe's seeing someone, also promising if she ever found out who it was . . . well, it wouldn't be pretty.

As Agatha sat staring at the rain, she could hear Gracie's voice. "I don't understand why you're telling me . . ."

Agatha turned, facing her. "Because I know it's you . . ."

Gracie paled, watching Agatha's eyes darken with intention. "I didn't . . ."

Agatha, however, was in no mood to listen. She shoved Gracie's shoulders hard, watching as her feet slipped in the snow to the river's edge. Moments later, Gracie floundered in the water, finally disappearing downstream.

It was that easy . . .

Until the following day when Gracie's body was discovered—it turned out the dorm receptionist had a propensity for gossip, and had no compunction about listening in on dormitory calls. She recalled the conversation perfectly, not hesitating to spill it when the cops came calling. "I knew something was up," she whispered, as if speaking words she shouldn't.

Still, Monroe stood by Agatha's side, refusing to believe any surfacing allegations. It wasn't long thereafter when the investigation slowly rolled to a stop, finally determining Gracie Brightwood slipped. An accident. Agatha steadfastly adhered to the story she left her friend alive and well and, as far as she knew, Gracie went back to her dorm.

Flimsy? Yes. But, apparently effective. Authorities called off their dogs, and the story of Gracie Brightwood faded, as did her light.

The rain steadily increasing, Agatha sat quietly, expressing no remorse. No tears for Gracie. No thoughts about a life snuffed out too early.

It's just the way it was . . .

CHAPTER

24

To surprise—Ryan insisted on going with Colbie for her interview with Morgan, not taking no for an answer. "There's no way on God's green earth I'm going to let you go alone—so, forget it!"

Naturally, there was no way Colbie could talk him out of it, so she settled for his agreeing to staying in the car. They perfected surveillance techniques when working their case in Cape Town, and he'd be ready if anything went south.

So would Dellinger—he, and undercovers would also be out of sight. He insisted, too.

The day dawned dark. Gloomy. Certainly fitting considering what Colbie had looming in front of her. Although she only knew of Morgan's reputation as a psychic, Colbie knew it would unwise to walk into a meeting without protecting herself.

She lay in bed, listening to the rain, allowing her body to relax, asking for her guides to be with her throughout the day, protecting her from dark energy. As she slipped into deep meditation, a voice she would always recognize surfaced—then, a soft hand on her face. "I will always love you, Colbie Colleen—but, now, it's time for you move on. You have much in front of you, and I'll be with you. Forever . . ."

Then, Brian kissed her lips gently for the last time.

CHAPTER

25

*A*s with Dellinger's and Baker's surprise visits to Buford and Beulah, Colbie's turning up on Morgan's doorstep unannounced left little time for a speedy exit out the back door—if there were one.

"This place looks creepier than the first time I was here," Ryan commented as they parked around the bend, out of sight.

But, Colbie didn't hear—she sat in the passenger's seat, eyes closed, opening her intuitive eye. It was prudent to go in with as much knowledge as possible, providing an opportunity to tap into Morgan within close proximity.

Ryan waited several minutes until she opened her eyes, taking a few seconds to reorient. "Her energy is so dark," Colbie finally commented. "But, at least I know . . ." A final check of the police wire, and she was out of the car, heading toward the spired fence. But, before Morgan's home came into view, she halted, again allowing her intuition to guide her—there was no doubt Morgan knew she was on her way.

Before she reached the porch steps, the door opened slowly. "I've been expecting you . . ."

Colbie stopped at the threshold. "I know . . ."

"Of course, I know why you're here." She stepped aside, gesturing to her guest to enter. "Please—make yourself comfortable."

Colbie wasn't sure what to expect, but, when she stepped inside, a warm, positive energy greeted her, welcoming her to a place where nature ruled, and energy worked for overall good. *Was I wrong about her?*

Morgan sat in a small, old-fashioned chair, Colbie choosing something not quite so comfortable. "So," Morgan began, "you want to know about Gracie Brightwood . . ."

So much for chitchat.

"Yes—I know you have specific information." Colbie hesitated for a moment. "I also know there was a pact between you, Beulah, and Buford Collins—and, authorities know, as well." Again, she paused. "So—you're in a rather precarious position, Ms. Stratford . . ."

"Morgan . . ."

Colbie nodded. "Morgan—the way I see it, you have a

decision to make. You see, I already know your involvement, but I need to hear it from you. The more you choose to say, the better things will be . . ."

The psychic focused her full attention on Colbie, weighing her words. "The only thing I'm guilty of is soaking Savannah's rich bitches for as much as they were willing to give—and, that was a lot . . ."

"When did you begin your . . . fruitful enterprise?"

"In my early twenties—it didn't take me long to recognize my abilities could play in my favor. As years passed, I attended parties—crashed, really—and, no one paid much attention to me until I did a reading or two on the Q.T." Morgan smiled. "It was simple—I chose my mark, then managed to insert myself into their lives. So much so, in fact, they couldn't imagine living without me . . ."

"Is that when you met Agatha?"

Morgan nodded. "And, Buford—although Beulah was the one who sent him to me. She knew how fragile he was, placing him in the position of the perfect foil for exacting revenge for her sister's murder . . ."

"Did you meet Agatha first?"

"Buford."

"How many times did you see him?"

"Well, if he didn't have a weekly appointment with me, I feared his going off the deep end . . ."

"And . . . that made it easy for you and Beulah to take advantage of his love for Gracie by convincing him Agatha Clyburn had to pay—isn't that right?"

"Indeed—although I had very little to do with it. I only listened as Buford carried Gracie's death with him for decades, and it wasn't until a year or so ago—maybe two— he began acting irrationally. Every time he came to me, he spoke of Gracie's haunting him—she came to him in dreams, asking him to act in her behalf . . ."

"What did that mean?"

Morgan looked at Colbie, slightly shocked. "Why, inflict the same pain on Agatha Clyburn! The same as she inflicted on him by killing his sister!"

"Did you put those ideas into his head?"

"Oh, no—that was all Beulah."

Colbie recalled Ryan's telling her about his conversation with Anna Lee Carlisle weeks prior—she made it a point to mention Beulah was a real piece of work. "Explain . . ."

"Somehow, Beulah knew Agatha murdered Gracie, although she never shared that information with me." She paused. "Who knows? Maybe she thought I already knew . . ."

Colbie thought for a moment. "So, what was the plan?"

"Get rid of Agatha's daughter—then, her husband. It was the only way, according to Beulah, Agatha could truly understand the agony she endured. Not to mention Buford's losing it . . ."

"An eye for an eye . . ."

"Yes . . . an eye for an eye."

"What about Buford?"

"Buford? He was to the point he'd believe anything— Beulah had him so convinced it was the only way he could prove his love for Gracie, and he'd do anything to stop his haunting dreams." Morgan focused her full attention on Colbie. "He was the key—without him, Beulah's plan wouldn't have worked."

Colbie glanced around the small front room, noting the energy was softer than when she walked in the door—an honest gentleness.

"Why? Why did you put yourself in such a position? You had to know what Beulah was planning was wrong—if she were playing Buford like a violin, she could certainly do the same to you. It looks as if you're going to pay the price . . ."

"Perhaps. But, it wasn't enough to dissuade me . . ."

"What was in it for you?"

"Money, of course!"

"Beulah paid you?"

Morgan laughed. "Oh, yes! Handsomely . . ."

Colbie didn't say anything, knowing Morgan would continue.

She did. "When it comes down to it, all I did was listen to Buford, telling him what dangers lurked before him. But, never once, did I suggest he bow to Beulah's suggestions. In fact, I warned him—though, I'm certain he didn't understand."

"Yes, but there's no denying you didn't try to talk him out of it . . ."

"True. However, attempting to do so would have been futile . . ."

Both women sat in silence for several minutes, each thinking of what was to come. Finally, Morgan spoke. "Will you please do me a favor, Ms. Colleen?"

For some reason, Colbie felt compelled to return Morgan's initial offer of familiarity. "Colbie . . ."

Morgan smiled. "Colbie—will you please disable the wire you're wearing?"

Trying not to show her surprise, Colbie thought for a moment, then complied, leaving Dellinger with nothing but an irritating crackle.

"Thank you. Now, I have a message for you . . ."

Colbie felt a warmth rush through her as she watched Morgan close her eyes.

"You recently suffered a loss," Morgan stated confidently.

"Yes . . ." Although it may seem impressive to some, Colbie knew Brian's perishing in the plane wreck was easily acquired information.

Morgan nodded slightly. "He's telling me he came to you this morning . . ."

Colbie sat, stunned.

"He wants me to tell you," Morgan continued, "to tell your partner he's sorry . . ."

Tears brimmed as Colbie thought about Ryan's not knowing Brian died. "Yes . . ." She could barely speak. There was no way Morgan Stratford could have known.

"He's sorry so much time passed after . . ." She paused. "I'm not sure what I'm seeing, but he's telling me it was a kidnapping . . ."

Colbie's heart ached as she listened.

"He wants your partner to know he'll always be with him . . ." Her eyelids fluttered open. "I know you'll convey the message." She paused, her face soft as she looked at Colbie. "And, you? He said his goodbye this morning . . ."

As they sat in momentary silence, Colbie felt a kinship with the woman who sat across from her. To receive such an intimate message from the other side was . . . well, an experience she never imagined. "I don't know what to say," she finally commented.

"You don't have to say anything . . ."

Colbie stood, then paused as she reached the door. "Thank you . . ." Then, she stepped outside to the first hint of a spring breeze, glancing at the sky.

She could feel his love.

.

CHAPTER

26

Not long after Colbie's interview with Morgan, Buford Collins went on the lam—subsequent interviews with Morgan revealed she severed all communication with Buford and Beulah, finally figuring out she was in a world of shit. Although there was little she could do to soften her position with Dellinger, refusing to accept Buford's calls gave, at least, the appearance of regretting her previous decisions.

It didn't take the detectives long to figure out without Beulah and Morgan as his anchors, Buford could no longer cope, and a non-extradition country proved tempting.

Beulah could have cared less, of course. She viewed Buford's actions as weak, and completely unbecoming behavior for anyone who may be in the presence of a Brightwood. Besides, she was much better off because he couldn't testify against her—unless they located him. Still, the whole thing was a sordid mess.

Morgan was in a slightly better position, but not much. She was up to her neck in the plan from the beginning and, if she would have kept her mouth shut when Colbie interviewed her, she might have been able to skate.

"She's a weird one, alright . . ." Damion picked up the bottle of merlot on the table, examining the label. "Your favorite?"

Colbie smiled. "Yep—it's about the only thing I drink!" She scanned the restaurant, knowing her days in Savannah were coming to an end. "How do you think everything's going to turn out?"

Dellinger topped off her glass. "Why don't you stay to find out?"

Colbie blushed. Although she enjoyed the attention, it felt strange—as if she were being unfaithful to Brian. "Damion . . ."

He noticed her unease. "Never mind—just wishful thinking, that's all . . ."

She appreciated his having the good taste to end the conversation and, for the next few hours, they swapped stories about investigations, Monroe's and Mariska's murders, and the possibility of Agatha's never going to trial for the murder of Gracie Brightwood.

Finally, however, it was time.

"If you find yourself in Savannah again, don't hesitate to look me up . . ."

Colbie grinned, then planted a gentle peck on his cheek. "You'll be the first to know . . ."

Then, she was gone.

CHAPTER

27

Although it seemed as if there shouldn't be much to do before leaving Savannah, Colbie and Ryan barely found enough time to discuss the future. It was clear both of them enjoyed working together, but, was it something they wanted to do on a permanent basis?

Neither were sure.

"We need to make flight arrangements . . ." Ryan glanced at Colbie, knowing she was ignoring tackling the subject neither one of them wanted to address. "So—how are you feeling about everything?"

She was quiet for a moment, then focused on the man who'd been by her side during the worst—if he'd have known Brian perished in the plane crash, he would have stood by her then, too. "I know I have to make a decision—but, to be honest, I'm not sure if I can go back to Seattle . . ."

Ryan nodded, knowing he didn't need to say anything.

"Everything's changed," she continued, "in ways I never dreamed possible. And, I'm not sure if I can handle it . . ."

"What is it you think you need to handle?"

"Walking into the house knowing Brian will never cross the threshold again . . ." She hesitated. "Knowing the future we planned will never be . . ."

Ryan watched as she slowly disintegrated, tears flowing freely.

"I should be moving on by now!"

"Who says? It seems to me you never allowed yourself the luxury of grieving . . ."

Silence.

"You know that never works . . ." He didn't take his eyes from her. "But, as much as it hurts, you're going to have to let go—that doesn't mean, however, you have to let go of your memories."

Colbie sniffled, then swiped at her nose with a tissue she had crammed in her pocket. "I know . . ."

Ryan went to her, pulled her up from her chair, then wrapped his arms around her. "It may not seem like much now, but you always have me . . ."

Colbie's cell buzzed as she was making a list of things she had to do before heading home. She glanced at the screen, surprised at name on her cell's caller I.D. "Damion?"

"I'll make it quick—Agatha Monroe wants to see you."

"What? Why?"

"She didn't say, but she's making some sort of ruckus at the loon . . . the hospital, and she says she won't stop until she speaks to you."

Colbie thought about the Clyburn matriarch, ideas swirling. "When?"

"As soon as you can get there . . ."

Moments later, armed with the address of the private mental facility more in keeping with Agatha's prior social stature, she signaled the only cab in front of her hotel—an hour later, sat next to her in a lovely, tapestry chair. There was little familiar about her—personal haunting made itself visible in her sunken eyes, and slightly ashen skin. In fact, if Colbie would have passed her on the street? She would have pegged her as one of Savannah's less fortunate.

"I'm sorry about Monroe," Colbie offered gently, unsure if she should begin the conversation.

Agatha looked at her, then focused her attention on something out the window. "Did you know Monroe was . . ." She hesitated. ". . . seeing someone?"

"I'm not sure what you mean . . ."

Agatha turned to her, eyes cold with disdain. "I mean exactly what I said—did you know Monroe was having an affair?"

Colbie hesitated, mentally cycling through her conversations with Monroe. "No, I didn't . . ."

"Oh, yes—for years. Seven, to be exact . . ."

Colbie wasn't sure what to say, although she suspected her comments didn't matter—clearly, it was Agatha's show.

"I should have known," Agatha continued. "He always had a predilection for wanting things he couldn't have. Gracie Brightwood was proof of that . . ."

Suddenly, Colbie realized why Agatha Culpepper Monroe summoned her. "What is it you need to tell me, Agatha?"

Agatha's eyes grew colder, if possible, ignoring Colbie's question. "Do you, Ms. Colleen, have any idea of who was keeping my husband's time?"

Colbie shook her head. "No . . ."

"Mary Ellen Beddington—that prim, little piece of fluff married to the dean of my alma mater!"

"How do you know?"

"Good heavens, don't be dense—what woman doesn't know when her husband is fooling around? Besides, it wasn't that difficult to figure out—one can only have so many evening meetings before curiosity tightens its grip."

"How long before you knew?"

Agatha turned to look at her momentarily, then again focused on the window. "Perhaps I was the one who was dense. It was nearly a year before I caught on . . ."

"Then what did you do—when you learned of Monroe's duplicity, I mean."

"Nothing." She glanced again at Colbie. "What was there to do? Divorce him? Good heavens—I had what I wanted, so there really was no need to rock the boat."

"Did you care?"

"Not really—after all, I had my children, and they were all I needed. Oh, I realize I wasn't the best mother—but, they wanted for nothing. Marcus, of course, took to my lifestyle better than Melbourne or Mariska, and I knew I could count on him for all of my needs—well, most of them."

Then, Colbie understood. "Tell me, Agatha, about the night of Monroe's murder . . ."

"What about it?"

"As I understand it, you weren't having the best evening—disturbing visions, I think."

"How do you know that?"

"It makes no difference how I know—what did you see?"

Agatha snorted a condescending laugh. "Nothing . . ."

Colbie knew that wasn't the truth—she also knew she was never going to get it. It was the perfect opportunity to turn the timbre of their conversation. "You set up Mary Ellen Beddington, didn't you?"

Agatha's eyes flashed with irrepressible anger. "I'm surprised you know—you didn't seem all that bright when you were conducting your investigation for Monroe . . ."

It was a stinging rebuke, one which Colbie had to ignore. "Well, both of us know forces were working against my determining the truth . . ."

"Perhaps . . ."

"So, how did you manage to acquire Mary Ellen Beddington's cell phone?"

Again, Agatha cackled, her true colors making their appearance. "She's such a . . . simple girl. Of course, I had no way of knowing Monroe's days were numbered, so, when I had the opportunity to chat with her at a social function, I made the best of it." She looked squarely at Colbie. "Her husband knew, as well . . ."

It was then Colbie knew for certain Agatha Clyburn had nothing to do with her husband's murder—her intent wasn't to kill him, but, rather, to make him pay dearly for the rest of their days together. Mary Ellen Beddington, too. Marcus and Melbourne gladly agreed to help when she told them of their father's disgraceful behavior, and it was Marcus enticing his father to the river on that frigid night. Melbourne, as it turned out, was totally worthless, reverting to his mouse-like personality the second he learned of his father's infidelity.

As she listened, Colbie knew Agatha had no clue about Buford. Or, Beulah. Or, the psychic encouraging Agatha to part with her money.

But, there was still the pesky case of Gracie Brightwood. "You know, of course, Beulah Brightwood holds you directly responsible for her sister's murder . . ."

"Of course, she does—there was no one else to blame, so she chose me . . ."

Colbie was quiet, keenly aware Agatha was parsing words—it seemed the best time for the direct approach. "But, it was you, wasn't it?"

Agatha stood, straightening her designer sweater. "I'm exhausted, I'm afraid . . ."

There was no mistaking—Colbie was dismissed.

News hit the airwaves the following day—Agatha Clyburn was deader than a doornail. Natural causes, they said, but Colbie wondered.

"It's pretty weird you saw her only yesterday," Ryan commented as they listened to evening reporters.

"No kidding—she didn't seem close to death, that's for sure!"

"When she kicked you to the curb yesterday, did you have any feeling she was mentally . . . compromised?"

Colbie shook her head. "No! Nothing!"

"When did she get rid of you?"

"When I asked her about Gracie Brightwood—it was pretty damned clear she didn't want to talk about it . . ."

"Then why did she call you over there?

"Simple—to tell me Monroe wasn't the saint everyone thought he was. He was a cheater, and she needed someone to know she fought back."

"Telling you was fighting back?"

"In a way—it was the one thing in her life over which she had control."

Ryan kicked off his shoes, then rested his feet on the coffee table. "Plus, my guess is she knew you figured out she was the one who murdered Gracie . . ."

"I think so—when I brought it up, that was all she wrote."

Ryan absentmindedly changed the channel, thinking about their case. "This is really going to frost Beulah, you know . . ."

"Well, it certainly doesn't speak well as reasons for her actions—no one can prove Agatha murdered Gracie, so, my guess is her murder will remain on the books."

"Beulah, Buford, and Morgan, however, are still on the hook for Mariska's and Monroe's murders . . ."

"Exactly—Agatha insisted Marcus had nothing to do with his father's death, so everything still points to Buford."

"We never did figure out the weird thing about Beddington's house—at least, where we thought he lived."

"I know—I have a feeling there's a lot more to Ernest Beddington than we'll ever know. I'm not sure I want to . . ."

They sat for a moment, thinking about the past year. It was one of the longest cases Colbie worked on and, since

Ryan worked with her in Cape Town—he'd experienced nothing like it.

He glanced at her. "So—this pretty much brings us full circle . . ."

"It seems so . . ."

"Are you going back to Seattle?"

"Yes—but only for a little while. I think I need a different place to land . . ."

"Any ideas as to where?"

"Not really . . ."

CHAPTER

28

*D*ellinger kept in touch throughout Beulah's and Morgan's trials, keeping her apprised of things news organizations didn't want to mention. There was a certain degree of celebrity when Morgan's trial rolled around and, as Colbie expected, she made the best of it. According to Damion, Savannah's psychic arrived at court looking exactly as she did for her readings—dressed in black, ears adorned with large, gold hoops, and rings on every finger, completing the picture. Within the year, both were sentenced to the murders of Mariska and Monroe Clyburn, and Colbie couldn't help but feel a twinge of regret—Morgan's motives were propelled by greed, but, Colbie felt she got in over her head.

Buford never did show his face in Savannah again, the doors to his company finally closing due to its becoming a rudderless, sinking ship.

Beulah, on the other hand, deserved everything she got.

After helping Colbie reorient in Seattle, Ryan returned to the East Coast, although he wasn't quite sure why. He and Colbie agreed to keep in touch and, of course, if he needed her to help on a case, he'd be more than happy.

That was two years prior. Now?

He needed her.

"Why on earth are you calling me so early?" Colbie glanced twice at the clock on her nightstand, making certain she read it correctly the first time.

"It's eight here—I've been up for hours!"

Colbie tried not to smile. "Well, bully for you!"

Ryan waited a second, listening to her prop the pillows. "You ready?"

"Yep—shoot!"

"Okay—ever since we worked the Savannah gig, things haven't been the same . . ."

"What do you mean?"

"Well—I've been working cases, but it kind of feels like something's missing."

"Such as?"

"Me. You. Kevin."

"Kevin?"

"Well—yeah! He was with us from the beginning, and I think he's perfect . . ."

Colbie wasn't sure she wanted to hear his answer, but she asked, anyway. "Perfect for what?"

"I think we need to form a new investigation firm—the three of us."

"What? Are you serious?"

"Of course, I'm serious! We make a good team!"

"Oh, I don't know, Ryan. I've been out of it for a while, and I'm not sure I want to dive back in the pool . . ."

"Why?"

Colbie hesitated, considering his question. It was one she didn't want to answer, but, at that moment, she knew she should. "I'm not sure I'm cut out for it, anymore. You know, after Brian . . ."

"I get it—but, it's been two years! How long are you going to carry the torch?"

Colbie gasped, disbelieving he could be so cruel. "I'm not carrying a torch!" Her face flamed with indignation. "How dare you!"

"I'm sorry—but, if you put down your pride for a minute, you'll see I'm right. You deserve more, Colbie! Brian's dead, and he wouldn't want you to pine for him! If there's anything I know about my best friend, it's that . . ."

Colbie was silent, deciding whether she wanted to continue the conversation—but, she knew she had to.

Tears choked her voice. "You're right . . ."

"Will you think about it?"

Silence.

"Colbie?"

"I'm here . . ."

"Well? Will you at least think about it? I really feel it's the right thing—the thought of talking to you about it has been eating me alive for months!"

"I'm that scary?"

"Damned straight you are!"

Another silence.

"So? What do you think? Colleen, Fitzpatrick, and Kevin—it has a ring to it!"

Colbie sighed and, as she did so, she felt the soft flutter of what she could only describe as wings. "Tell me what you have in mind . . ."

And, so it went.

Life changed for three people who were meant to be together, yet they didn't know it until Colbie's tragedy consumed them—even then, they weren't too quick on the uptake. But, as usually happens, the situation righted itself and, by the time summer was on the cusp, they had their first, official work meeting. Ryan and Kevin relocated temporarily to Seattle, agreeing with Colbie they needed to choose where they wanted to land permanently. It was an unorthodox way of handling a new partnership, but, it worked, and there was a positive anticipation none felt for a long time.

Kevin was beside himself as he sat with his new partners ready to give his all to their new venture. Since his unfortunate dismissal from Monroe Pharmaceuticals, he managed to hang in there with typical, boring jobs, but, in his heart he knew there was something more he should do. It wasn't until Colbie and Ryan called offering him their opportunity, did he understand the true meaning of serendipity. "I can't believe I'm here," he commented. "I never thought in a million years when I met you a few years ago, I'd be starting a new life . . ."

Ryan grinned. "I know what you mean! I did the same thing many years ago—and, I never figured Colbie and I would be working together as partners . . ."

"Okay, gentlemen—how about if we get down to business?" There was no doubt who was running the show. "First up—where we want to set up shop permanently?"

As far as Kevin was concerned, they could work in a closet, and he'd be happy. Besides, he didn't know enough to offer an opinion, so he figured it best if he took a back seat. "I'm game for anywhere—whatever you guys decide, I'm in!"

Colbie and Ryan glanced at each other, both enjoying Kevin's enthusiasm. "Fair enough," Ryan agreed. "I guess we need to first figure out whether we're staying stateside . . ."

"True. Or, we can choose international . . ." She focused on Kevin. "Do you have a passport?"

He nodded. "Yep—ever since I was fifteen!"

For the next few hours, they hashed out states and countries, finally deciding international was the wisest choice. "Now, all we have to do is finalize—any votes for London?"

None.

"France?" Ryan took a swig of coffee, glancing at Kevin— clearly, they were holding out.

Colbie laughed. "Okay! I get it! Switzerland it is!"

"What's the official company name?"

"Good question . . ."

"I take it you didn't like my suggestion of 'Colleen, Fitzpatrick, and Kevin' . . ."

After bandying several names back and forth, all realized it was prudent to stick with something simple. "How about CFK International Investigations," Kevin asked. "And, if anyone asks what the 'K' stands for, we'll tell 'em!"

Colbie and Ryan stared at him. "Is it really that simple," Ryan asked, laughing.

"Apparently!" Colbie sat back, enjoying the camaraderie.

It had been a long time.

Their new office was small, but, as Ryan pointed out on several occasions, they really didn't need much—if Colbie could spearhead her business from her home in Seattle, palatial digs weren't necessary.

Although one of Colbie's cases several years prior took her to Zurich, after two recon trips, they decided on settling in Geneva. Kevin's only issue was language—with French, German, and Italian widely spoken throughout the country, English wasn't nearly as popular, and he feared he wouldn't communicate well. He figured it wouldn't make a difference for his personal life, but, when it came to business? He didn't want to sound like an idiot. So, Colbie sprang for top-notch language software and, within a few months, he could carry on brief conversations—which, as it turned out, played in their favor when word got out Colbie Colleen was a resident.

That's when it got tricky.

After Brian's passing, Colbie took a well-deserved hiatus from work—two years—and, her name fell off potential clients' radar. Of course, she wasn't exactly starting over, but she did need to expend considerable effort. It was a situation proving difficult—she only agreed to Ryan's suggestion of becoming partners because she felt mired in a life she knew was mentally unhealthy. Still, for all of her training and education, she descended into depression, allowing no one to see. No one to feel her grief with her.

No one to care.

For two years, she lived in her shadow world, only surfacing when she felt no one was looking. She suspected

Ryan knew—how could he not? He remained silent, however, allowing her the time she needed to resolve her demons. Yet, doing so took her to places she didn't want to go. It was hard knowing the last time she was in Switzerland, she and Brian were working together and, in some ways, it wasn't fair to Ryan. Without knowing it, she was expecting him to fill shoes he couldn't.

It was, without question, an impossible task.

"Colbie?" Ryan popped his head in her tiny office, a grin plastered on his face. "Got a minute?"

"When wouldn't I have a minute? We haven't been that busy!" She laughed, closing her laptop. "What's up?"

"A new client. Maybe . . ."

"Seriously?"

"Yep—just got off the phone with him."

Colbie sat back in her chair. "Well? Don't keep me in suspense!"

Ryan took his time checking two pages of notes—just to drive her crazy, of course. "Okay—it sounds complicated, but I think it's right up our alley . . ."

"And . . ."

"Think fashion . . ."

"Fashion? You mean high fashion?"

"Yep—about the highest you can think of!"

Colbie was quiet for a moment as she considered the possibilities. "Well—the first thing I think of is Paris. Or, Rome . . ."

"Don't forget Milan . . ."

"Right . . . so, what about them?"

Ryan enjoyed every second of stringing her along, knowing full well their possible new case was exactly the type of case she enjoyed. "Okay—you have those cities in mind, right? Now, think drugs . . ."

"Drugs within the fashion industry? That's not news . . ."

"True. But, couple that with jewel thefts? Diamonds? Sounds like news to me . . ."

Again, Colbie was silent. Then she stood, crossing to one of two tiny windows, staring at those on the street, thoughts swirling.

Finally, she turned to Ryan. "It sounds like the intersection of blood and money to me . . ."

NOVELS BY AWARD-WINNING AUTHOR,
FAITH WOOD!

the Accidental Audience—Book I
a Colbie Colleen Cozy, Suspense Mystery

Chasing Rhinos—Book 2
a Colbie Colleen Cozy, Suspense Mystery

Apology Accepted—Book 3
a Colbie Colleen Cozy, Suspense Mystery

Whiskey Snow—Book 4
a Colbie Colleen Cozy, Suspense Mystery

LAUNCHING IN SPRING, 2019!

At the Intersection of Blood and Money—Book 6
a Colbie Colleen Cozy, Suspense Mystery

ABOUT THE AUTHOR

Faith Wood is a Behaviorist, Certified Professional Speaker, Hypnotist, and Handwriting Analyst. Her interest in Behavior Psychology blossomed during her law enforcement career when it occurred to her if she knew what people really wanted, as well as motives behind their actions, she would be more effective in work and life. So, she hung up her cuffs, trading them in for traveling the world speaking to audiences to help them better understand human behaviors, and how they impact others. Wood speaks about how to tap into the area of the brain controlling actions which, in turn, have a tendency to adjust perceptions, thereby launching a more empowered life.

A mother of four, she lives with her husband in British Columbia, Canada.

ACKNOWLEDGMENTS

My most sincere thanks to everyone who sticks with me through the days when I wonder what to write next—you never fail me!

Many thanks to my editor, Laurie—she and her team get it done right every time!

Finally—to my family. Always there, always cheering me on. I couldn't be more grateful . . .

PROFESSIONAL ACKNOWLEDGMENTS

CHRYSALIS PUBLISHING AUTHOR SERVICES
L.A. O'NEIL, Editor
www.chrysalis-pub.com
chrysalispub@gmail.com

HIGH MOUNTAIN DESIGN
WYATT ILSLEY, Cover Design
www.highmountaindesign.com
hmdesign89@gmail.com

69901120R00161

Made in the USA
Middletown, DE
23 September 2019